THE NEWLYWED'S LIE

ZIA RAYYAN

Copyright © 2025 by Zia Rayyan

All rights reserved.

No part of this book may be reproduced in any form or by any electronic or mechanical means, including information storage and retrieval systems, without written permission from the author, except for the use of brief quotations in a book review.

AUTHOR'S NOTE

Though this book is a work of fiction, it does take place in Cascais, Portugal, which is a very real city. I've done my best to portray elements of Portuguese society and culture with respect and care, but I do recognize the limits of my own perspective and ability. Any inaccuracies are unintentional, and come from a place of love.

ONE
MORGAN

It's funny how no book ever talks about what comes after a happy ending.

I'm not sure why I never thought about it before, despite having shelved so many books as a librarian. But now I realize there's a good reason for that. Happy endings are temporary. The moment someone is dragged back into life's dull monotony, their story turns to misery.

Misery. That's exactly the word for what I'm feeling at the moment.

My leg throbs as I push aside the stolen blanket and stuff it into the bag I'd been using as a pillow. My back aches from sleeping on the cobblestones of the alley. It's not like I have a choice. I just arrived illegally in not only the country but one of its most expensive seaside cities.

Cascais.

Even through my exhaustion, Cascais mocks me with its beauty. Pastel buildings catching the morning light while I huddle in their shadows, bougainvillea blooming in violent pinks and purples while I wilt in yesterday's stolen clothes.

It's easy to see why Henry loved this place. It's not just about how beautiful it is. It's about the people. Here, they wake up to feel alive, to take joy in the beauty of the ocean and the culture surrounding them. It's far different from back home, where people just wake up to slap their alarm clocks into silence and stumble toward another day of slow death.

I have a feeling I could love Cascais too.

That is, if I could get some food in my belly and some cash in my pocket. I push the thought aside, forcing myself to stay positive. Because here's the reality: I'm the only one alive with a reason to care about me. Everyone else who ever loved me is dead.

My mother, my father, and now... Henry.

Well, maybe.

Who's to say that bastard ever loved me in the first place?

I brace my hand against the alley wall, feeling the cold seep through my palm as I force myself upright. My joints protest with a sharp, vindictive pain that shoots up my spine like lightning. The kind of pain that makes you understand why people break when they're pushed too far. It'll fade once I get moving. I know this by now. And right now, only one thing matters.

Finding someone who'll give me an off-the-books job, enough to get a roof over my head. I don't have a work visa or the means to file for one. That leaves me stuck.

After stretching each protesting muscle, I find the strength to leave my makeshift shelter. The morning breeze carries the scent of fresh bread and espresso from nearby cafés.

My stomach twists in hunger. Another reason to be miserable. Yet for the first time in days, something close to hope stirs in my chest.

Today will be different. It has to be.

That hope doesn't live long, because that's when I hear it.

"—crackdown starts next week," a woman's voice says in accented English. "Police will be doing sweeps every morning. No more sleeping rough in the city center."

My blood turns to ice. I slow my pace, pretending to window-shop while straining to hear more.

"About time," her friend says. "These tourists come here expecting paradise, not to step over homeless people."

The woman laughs. "The mayor says it's for public health and safety, but we all know it's about the tourism dollars."

I force myself to keep walking. Time is running out. I could leave. Pack my few stolen belongings and catch the first train to somewhere cheaper, somewhere I'd have an easier time of starting a new life. Spain, maybe. Or further inland, where the cost of living won't bleed me dry. The rational choice is obvious.

But my feet carry me deeper into the city instead, toward the harbor where cruise ships dock. Where tourists arrive from all over the world. Where someone like Henry might have brought his real wife on their honeymoon.

Truth is, I know exactly why I'm staying, and I hate myself for it.

It's not the city's beauty that keeps me here. Not even the desperate hope of finding work. It's the pathetic fantasy that someday, somehow, he might come back. That I might see him walking these streets, and I could... what? Confront him? Beg him to tell me if any of it was real?

Even knowing everything now—that I was nothing but a therapeutic tool, a human prop in Eden's plan to save Henry and Genevieve's marriage—some twisted part of me still loves him. Still wants to believe that what I felt in his arms meant something.

Like I said before...

Misery.

TWO
MORGAN

Every step sends shooting pain up my leg. I grit my teeth and force myself forward, knowing that while rest would be better for my injured leg, I simply can't afford to stop. It doesn't stop me from cursing Genevieve's name for the stray shot though.

But it'll heal. All things do, with time. Or at least, that's what I tell myself when the throbbing pain shifts from my leg to my heart.

The tourist map in my hands shows locations crossed out with angry X's for every place that turned me away when I asked for side work. At this point, most of my map looks like a tic-tac-toe board where no one won. But there are still a few places left to try.

Including a café that sits perched on one of the cliffsides. Henry once mentioned his love for one, but unfortunately, there's no way to tell which one it was; there are more than a dozen scattered along the coastline. Every evening, you can see tourists camped at their tables, phones raised to capture the sun melting into the horizon.

My gaze lands on the name of a café that's further away than most of the places I've tried so far.

Café do Horizonte.

The name sounds promising enough.

Step by agonizing step, I follow the winding cobblestone path upward. The incline makes my injured leg scream in protest, and it takes me the better part of an hour to reach the entrance. I try not to think about the journey back down if this place rejects me as well.

The café unfolds before me like something from a postcard: white-washed walls, blue shutters, tables scattered across a stone terrace that juts out over the cliff. The ocean stretches endlessly below, painted in shades of amber and rose by the rising sun.

A beautiful woman with dark hair moves gracefully from table to table in a long, flowing dress that catches the breeze, refilling glasses and collecting empty plates. Near the entrance, I smooth down my hair and tuck away the worst wrinkles in my stolen shirt. When she finally notices me, she approaches with a warm smile.

She doesn't bother with Portuguese. I'm guessing I give off that American energy. But there's no judgment in her dark eyes, only kindness. "Table just for one?"

"Actually, I... I'm hoping I can work for you."

Her smile falters, confusion flickering across her features. "Work? You want to work here?"

I nod, straightening my shoulders and trying to hide the hint of desperation in my voice. "I need money, but I don't want to beg. I want to earn it."

She shakes her head sadly. "Sorry, there is no work here."

I close my eyes, that fragile thread of hope snapping inside my chest. It's only my first stop of the day, but already I feel drained at the thought of limping all the way back down into the town center.

My stomach growls loudly enough that a couple at a nearby table glances over, their lips curling at the sight of me.

The woman's eyes flick down to the sound, then back to meet mine. There's a warmth there, a kind understanding that even if she can't offer me work, she recognizes the desperate situation I'm in.

"Thank you anyway," I say. She could have been far harsher in rejecting me. God knows I've experienced that already from half the restaurants and shops I've approached. I turn to go, but her voice stops me.

"Do you want food?"

I look back over my shoulder.

"You eat?" She motions with her hand, gesturing toward an empty table positioned right along the edge of the terrace.

I shouldn't. I should stay focused on finding work that'll put money in my pocket so I can afford my own meals. But it's hard to deny the gnawing hunger and the desert dryness of my throat. I can practically taste the fresh orange juice gleaming in a glass at a nearby table. My eyes well with tears as I slowly nod.

She leads me to the table, her dress billowing as she pulls out a chair that faces the endless expanse of ocean. The wind catches my hair, lifting it away from my face for the first time in days. I settle into the seat, trying to ignore the disapproving glances from a cluster of locals at a corner table. Well-dressed women who shake their heads and whisper behind their hands.

"I bring you food," the woman says warmly. "Something nice, okay?"

"Could I... if it's possible, could I have some orange juice?" The words come out smaller than I mean for them to.

She smiles and nods. "Sim, claro. Of course."

As she disappears back into the café, I catch fragments of conversation from the women behind me, their voices drifting between Portuguese and heavily accented English.

"I do not understand why these tourists, they try to make life here. No família, no friends, nada. What kind of home can be this without these things?"

The other woman snorts. "You know the woman who owns the blue house near the marina? Twenty years she's been here, but still she acts like turista. Some people, they never learn. You cannot build life on someone else's life."

"Verdade."

Truth. The word surfaces in my mind automatically now, after weeks of immersion.

The woman wipes her mouth with a napkin and folds it over her lap, pursing her lips. She flashes a glare in my direction, before continuing. "They come and buy our houses with their money, then leave and never return. Why? Because these are not real homes when you have nothing of your own inside them. But when they go, our properties? They stay in their names para sempre."

"Malditos turistas," the other mutters under her breath. I'd heard that phrase enough around town to know it meant 'damn tourists.' People weren't shy about using it when they thought I couldn't understand.

The kind woman returns with a tall glass of fresh orange juice and catches me listening. She sets the glass down with a gentle smile. "They come every day. Always complaining. Every day, the same. You ignore them, okay? They are upset because the beautiful houses like the mansions, they stay empty."

The woman gestures vaguely toward the coastline, where mansions dot the highest cliffs.

"That one there," she says, pointing to a sprawling white villa perched at the highest point overlooking the bay, "it belongs to some rich businessman from America. Beautiful, não? But he has not been seen for many years."

I follow her gaze upward, taking in the elegant lines of the structure, all clean angles and expansive terraces that seem to float above the ocean. Floor-to-ceiling windows catch the morning light, and I can just make out the edge of what looks like an infinity pool. Even from this distance, it's breathtaking.

"Must be nice," I murmur, more to myself than to her.

She nods sympathetically. "Many houses like this here. Rich people, they buy but never come. Meanwhile, locals struggle to buy homes." She shrugs, the gesture holding years of resigned frustration. "But what can we do?"

She leaves and returns a few moments later with the food. It's a simple but perfect plate of scrambled eggs, fresh bread with butter and jam, and a small pastry that looks like a mini croissant. My mouth waters as she sets it down, along with a small bowl of olives, that blessed glass of orange juice, and a steaming cup of coffee that smells like heaven.

It's enough to make my eyes well with tears when I look up at her. "Obrigado."

It's one of the few Portuguese words I've heard. Thank you.

She beams at my attempt, but then leans forward and says, "*Obrigada,* for women."

"Obrigada," My cheeks burn as I repeat after her, feeling like a small child. But I remind myself that learning a language is hard, and is meant to be humbling.

"Good." She pats my shoulder and smiles at me. "Now enjoy."

I tear into the meal with embarrassing enthusiasm, trying to pace myself but failing miserably. The pastry flakes apart under my fork, seasoned with something I can't identify but desperately want to learn about. The orange juice is fresh-squeezed and tart, washing away the bitter taste of disappointment that's been coating my tongue for days. And the coffee? It's morphine for all the pain I've suffered since I left home.

As I eat, my eyes keep drifting back to that mansion on the cliff. What would it be like to have a place like that? Somewhere I could lock the door and feel safe, where I could heal properly instead of constantly looking over my shoulder.

A dangerous thought enters my mind, and I push it away. But I can't stop myself from imagining what it would feel like to wake up in those sun-soaked rooms and to finally exhale, knowing that I had a foundation to build a life upon.

Barely half an hour passes by the time I finish every crumb of my meal, without so much as a single drop of orange juice or coffee left.

The woman comes to take my plates, gently shooing me away when I try to stack the plates. I watch her work, and it's strange... I feel a connection to her that I haven't felt with anybody else so far.

Maybe it's the kindness she's shown me.

Either way, I find myself tapping her on the shoulder. "I... My name is Morgan."

She smiles and presses a hand to her chest. "Catarina. You are welcome, Morgan."

When she leaves with the dishes in hand, I push the chair back and stand. I wince as I feel a jolt of pain, reminding me of the long, dreadful path back.

I spare one last look for the beautiful, empty mansion. A life like that would've been mine if my marriage to Henry had survived. If *he* survived.

Instead, it seems I'm meant for something else. A job, hopefully. I shake my head and step back onto the cobblestone path, waving another thank you to Catarina.

Somewhere in this picturesque coastal town, there has to be someone willing to give a poor, injured American a chance.

Even if I have no idea what I'm qualified to do besides organize books, dream of houses I'll never afford, and survive deadly marriage therapy programs.

THREE
HENRY

You know what I love about money?

It can get you access to just about anything you want. State-of-the-art experimental healthcare so advanced and expensive that even politicians can't access it. It's all about how much you have and how much you're willing to spend.

And I'm willing to spend it all to get back on my feet faster. Between the multiple bone fractures, the concussion, the internal bleeding, and the gunshot wound, I was expected to be out of commission for at least four to six months. Maybe longer, considering the rehabilitation I'd need to walk again. But that's in a *normal* hospital, and I won't wait that long.

Somewhere out there is the love of my life. And every day that passes is another day she gets closer to moving on. After all, I'm supposed to be dead. It's a miracle that I survived the fall from the cliff, let alone all the jagged rocks jutting out like teeth along the cliffside.

But I'm not dead. I'm alive. I'm very much alive, and I

can't handle the idea that she might trust her heart to someone else to help her heal from all of this.

As her husband, that's *my* job.

Or at least, it will be once I get out of here, find her, and finish my vows.

It shouldn't be much longer now. The doctors said that with the experimental treatment, recovery time should be closer to three weeks. Four at most.

I can handle that long.

The IV drip beside my bed hums its mechanical rhythm, pumping thousands of dollars worth of synthetic healing into my bloodstream. The private suite smells like expensive disinfectant and imported Egyptian cotton sheets. Nothing like the antiseptic stench of regular hospitals. Even the monitors beeping around me are sleek and silent, their displays showing vital signs that would normally take weeks to achieve.

But none of it can stop the craving that claws at my throat. My fingers twitch against the silk bedding, muscle memory reaching for a pack that isn't there. The phantom taste of tobacco coats my tongue, and I can almost feel the burn of smoke filling my lungs. My left hand trembles—not from the injuries, but from withdrawal that makes my skin crawl and my jaw clench.

God, what I wouldn't give for just one drag. Just one moment of that perfect clarity that only nicotine can provide.

The craving mingles with the fire racing through my bones, and I force myself to focus on what matters. Morgan. Where she is, what she's doing, whether she's mourning me or moving on.

Morgan can be quite predictable. Sure, she surprised me on the island with everything that happened, but I know how her mind works. She'll seek out comfort in the only way she knows how. The good thing is that while I may not yet know what I'm going to say to her, I do know exactly where she'll go.

And when I'm able, I'll find her.

FOUR
MORGAN

"Check over there."

A man's voice echoes through the alley, startling me awake. Exhaustion tries to drag me back under, but I can't ignore the spike of adrenaline flooding my system. Something's wrong.

I press my hand against the cold stone wall and push myself upright, every bone and muscle screaming in protest. Moving as quietly as I can, I shift forward and peer around the corner of the alley.

I freeze.

Police. Portuguese voices, official badges, the whole terrifying package. Has a week passed already? The days have been blurring together. Endless rejections from shops and restaurants broken up only by the occasional reprieve when I could make it up the cliff to Café do Horizonte for a friendly chat and meal with Catarina.

The Cascais officers move with practiced efficiency, checking doorways and alcoves with the systematic thoroughness of people who've done this sweep a hundred times before. They know exactly where people like me try to sleep.

I scramble back to my bag, shoving the thin blanket inside and slinging it over my shoulder just as one of the officers shouts from behind.

"Espera aí!"

The wind roars in my ears as I take off running, sharp bolts of pain shooting up my injured leg with every step. It feels like I'm flying, but I know the truth. If these officers really wanted to catch me, they could. I'm not exactly athletic. Shoot, I was always picked last for every sport in high school, more comfortable with books than anything requiring coordination.

Something I'm brutally reminded of when my lungs finally surrender and force me to stop, pain clenching my side like a vise. I bend over, gasping for air, my mouth flooding with saliva as I try not to vomit.

This is just the beginning of the crackdown. The Cascais police will go easy for a few days, scare enough people to either chase them out of the area or force them into legitimate work before they start making actual arrests. And I'm definitely not prison material. There aren't nearly enough books in there to keep me sane. I'd go crazy.

I force myself to keep walking, staying to the smaller side streets where the shadows are deeper and the chance of running into another patrol is lower. My bag feels heavier with each step, the strap cutting into my shoulder.

The early morning light is starting to creep across the cobblestones, painting everything in shades of gray that match my mood perfectly. Soon, the shopkeepers will start opening their doors, the café owners will flip their signs, and I'll have to face another day of rejections and barely concealed disgust.

How many times can you hear "Não, desculpe" before it stops feeling like an apologetic rejection and starts feeling like a death sentence?

I think about Catarina, probably already starting her morning prep at the café. The one bright spot in this endless nightmare. But even her kindness has limits, and I can see the worry in her eyes when I show up looking more ragged each day. How long before she stops offering me food? How long before she realizes I'm not just a tourist having a rough patch, but someone that might drive away her customers?

The thought makes my chest tighten with a familiar panic. I'm running out of options, running out of time, running out of the stubborn hope that's kept me going since I arrived in this postcard-perfect town that's become my personal hell.

I turn down another narrow street, this one lined with shuttered shops that won't open for hours. A bakery with flour-dusted windows. A bookstore that makes my heart ache with longing for all those stories I can't afford to lose myself in anymore. A small pharmacy with a hand-written sign I can't read but recognize as another closed door.

That's when I see it.

Just a glimpse between two buildings, but enough to make me stop walking. The mansion on the cliff, that beautiful white villa Catarina had pointed out that day we met. Even from this distance, even partially hidden by the morning haze, it looks like something from a dream.

Its owner hasn't been back for many years. That's what she said.

I stare at it, my heart doing something strange in my chest. Not hope, exactly—I've learned not to trust that feeling anymore. But something else.

What if?

The thought comes unbidden, dangerous as a loaded gun. I push it away, but it keeps creeping back. Empty houses don't stay empty forever, but they can stay empty long enough. Long enough for someone to figure out their next move.

I know what I'm thinking is insane. Breaking into someone's house—someone rich enough to own a cliffside mansion in one of Portugal's most expensive coastal towns—isn't just desperate. It's criminal. The kind of criminal that gets you deported if you're lucky, and imprisoned for *years* if you're not.

But what's the alternative? Try to make it back to the States with no money, no ID, no anything? How long would it be before Eden found me and killed me to keep me quiet? I still don't know if they're searching for me or not.

I can't keep sleeping in alleys either, because it's only a matter of time until the police catch me. And it's not like I can snap my fingers and change my situation. There's a reason nobody's giving me a job, beyond the fact that I'm an unskilled illegal immigrant who doesn't even speak Portuguese. It's because I look and smell like a vagrant.

No, they would only ever give a chance to someone who is clean and approachable. Someone who's recently *showered*.

God... I bet that mansion has at least seven showers. One I could use for every day of the week.

It's that thought that finally has me adjusting my bag and walking again, this time with purpose. The streets of Cascais wind upward as they approach the cliffs, getting narrower and more residential. The houses here are older, more weathered, built for locals rather than tourists. I pass gardens overgrown with bougainvillea, their bright purple flowers contrasting with the surrounding gray stone walls.

The climb is brutal on my injured leg, but I grit my teeth and keep going. Every step takes me higher, closer to that gleaming white villa that represents either salvation or the stupidest decision I've ever made.

Probably both.

The streets get quieter as I climb, the tourist crowds replaced by the occasional local walking a small dog or carrying groceries. I keep my head down, trying to look like I belong here, like I have every right to be wandering through their neighborhood at dawn, though nothing could be further from the truth.

By the time I reach the level where the mansion sits, my leg is screaming and my lungs are burning. But there it is, even more beautiful up close than it had looked from a distance. Three stories of pristine white stone, floor-to-ceiling windows that reflect the morning sky, and that infinity pool I'd glimpsed from Catarina's café.

The property is surrounded by a high stone wall

topped with decorative ironwork expensive enough to keep out casual intruders, but not impossible to climb.

I walk the perimeter slowly, trying to look like someone out for a morning stroll rather than someone casing the joint. The back of the property faces the cliff, offering the kind of privacy that wealthy people pay millions for. It also means there are no neighbors with a direct line of sight to whatever might happen in the next few hours.

Perfect.

I find what I'm looking for near the corner where the wall meets a cluster of pine trees. The stones are older here, with more gaps between them, and the ironwork on top is purely decorative: beautiful scrollwork that wouldn't stop a determined child, let alone a desperate adult.

My hands are shaking as I tighten my bag on my shoulder and test the first handhold. The stone is solid, warm from yesterday's sun, and rough enough to provide good grip. I can do this. I have to do this.

One way or another, I'm not spending another night in an alley.

I take a deep breath, taste salt air and the faint scent of jasmine from someone's garden, and begin to climb.

FIVE
MORGAN

I hit the ground hard, a wheezing gasp escaping my lips as my leg folds and I collapse onto soft grass. Blackness swims at the edges of my vision. It's all I can do to keep from screaming as my leg tightens with pain. It feels just as bad as when I got shot.

I wait for the pain to dull, its throbbing subsiding as one minute passes, then two, then five. I don't know how long I stay there, lying in the grass and staring up at the sky with tears in my eyes. But it's long enough that by the time I get to my feet, the sun's halfway up the sky.

Running my hand through my tangled hair, I pick my bag up off the ground and start limping toward the house.

Up close, it's even more stunning than I'd imagined. The white stone walls gleam in the morning light. Three stories of Mediterranean elegance rise before me, with expansive terraces that seem to float above the cliff. Floor-to-ceiling windows reflect the ocean like mirrors, and the infinity pool… it reminds me of the sort of thing that influencers would kill to have access to.

And beyond it all is an endless expanse of blue stretching far to the horizon. This isn't just wealth. This is the kind of generational money that builds monuments to itself.

I creep closer to the nearest window, cupping my hands against the glass to peer inside. The room beyond is filled with leather furniture that probably costs more than I made in a year at the library. But that's not what steals my breath away. It's the bookshelves lining the walls. And they are filled with books.

I can tell that whoever owned this house must be a reader, because the spines don't look like what you'd expect of a typical wealthy person: leather-bound books containing every word of law, classics that make you seem educated when the spines don't show a single sign of ever being opened. No, these are modern-day novels. I can't make out the titles, but by the design of them, it looks like a healthy mixture of thrillers, fantasy, and even romance.

I have to get in.

I tear my eyes away from the bookshelves, searching for some sign of life. But the silence is absolute. No distant music or laughter. Not even the hum of air conditioning can be heard, although I suppose rich people can probably afford better quality stuff than I'm used to.

The place looks entirely empty.

My mouth curves upward at the thought of having this whole place to myself. I've never been one to covet mansions. Back in Iowa, they just seemed like expensive, soulless prisons. But standing here in front of one, I can't deny the appeal. It's beautiful, peaceful, private, and that *library*.

It's then that I notice a little blinking light on a box mounted to the wall.

Security.

How the hell could I have been so *stupid*? Of course a place like this would have an alarm system. What mansion didn't? Rich people don't leave millions of dollars' worth of property unguarded.

The second I break in, the owner will get some sort of notification and it wouldn't be long until the Cascais police shows up with their guns drawn and handcuffs ready. I'd go from homeless beggar to international criminal in the span of a morning.

I grind the heels of my palms against my forehead, feeling like the world's biggest idiot. But even as I berate myself, I push past the self-doubt and lean into the desperate hope that's kept me alive this long. Maybe the owner wouldn't notice the notification of a break in. Or maybe, just maybe, the security system is deactivated.

Crazier things have happened in the world, right? I mean, supposedly all those cameras were down in a *maximum security prison* whenever Epstein somehow "hung" himself. If that could happen, then it's certainly possible that this security system was... also not working?

It's a stretch, I know, but the thought takes the edge off my panic. It gives me something to hope for as I circle around to the front door.

The entrance is imposing. Heavy wooden doors with ornate brass hardware that's probably worth more than most people's cars. There's a keypad beside the door, its little red light blinking like it knows I'm not supposed to be here.

I shake my head and absentmindedly try the door handle, not really expecting it to turn. Except it does, and the door swings open fast enough that I nearly fall flat onto my face.

Shocked, I straighten myself and stare into the entryway. That felt too easy. But maybe the universe thinks I've had it hard enough lately. Maybe I'm overdue a little luck.

It's amazing how much I've changed in such little time. Not too long ago, I would have balked at the idea of breaking in someplace. And only just recently, I'd broken in and planted a note in Genevieve's suite that ultimately led to her—and Henry's—deaths.

I'm a different person now. For all the horror that I suffered on that island, it made me stronger. It made me a survivor. Someone who doesn't really need luck at all.

I steel my jaw, sling my bag off my shoulder, and reach inside. There were only two things I kept when I stepped off the private jet.

The first was the ring that Henry slid over my finger. It's hidden safely away in a pocket in my bag. The smart thing to do would be to sell it and set myself up with that money. But for some reason, I just can't do it.

And the second thing I kept?

My hand closes around the steel handle of a gun. The same gun that I used in my escape off the island. The same one that Genevieve used to kill my traitor of a husband, Henry.

Taking a deep breath, I switch the safety off and enter the house.

The silence inside is deafening. My footsteps echo

against marble floors as I step into the foyer, the gun heavy in my hand. I pause just inside the doorway, listening for any sounds of life. But there's nothing. No steady hum of a refrigerator, no ticking clocks, no voices. Just the distant crash of waves against the cliff below and my own ragged breathing.

The entryway opens into a grand hallway that stretches toward the back of the house. To my right, I can see the library I'd glimpsed through the window. The books call to me, but I force myself to stay focused. First, I need to make sure I'm alone.

I move deeper into the house.

The hallway opens into a massive guest area with soaring ceilings and floor-to-ceiling windows that frame the ocean like a living painting. The furniture is elegant but comfortable-looking: cream-colored sofas arranged around a coffee table made from what looks like a single piece of driftwood.

Despite the tension in my shoulders, I can't help but feel a flutter of excitement at the idea of curling up here with a book, safe and clean and warm, watching the sun set over the ocean.

I head into the main living area. It seems to be the only room without a massive view of the ocean. In fact, there aren't many windows at all.

With the sudden absence of light making it seem so much darker, I flick the switch and jump as a sudden fire roars to life underneath the mantelpiece.

Warmth and light blooms across the darkness, transforming the room into something far more welcoming and comforting.

A line of framed photographs pulls me forward, and as I approach, I lower the gun.

The first photo shows a Portuguese woman with dark hair and kind eyes. She's laughing at something off-camera, her whole face lit up with joy.

The second photo is of the same woman with a little girl, maybe two years old, with gray eyes and dark hair. They're grinning at the camera. They're on a beach somewhere.

I pick up the frame, studying their faces. This house must belong to them. But didn't Catarina say that the house belonged to some American?

I put the photo back and glance toward the third frame.

My blood turns to ice.

It's Henry.

He's standing on what looks like the same beach from the mother-daughter photo, his arm around the Portuguese woman. They're both laughing.

The gun slips from my numb fingers, clattering to the marble floor. Shaking, I reach for the photo, hoping that I'm mistaken.

I'm not.

The photo wasn't taken recently, but while he may not have the same mature definition in his face, I can tell that it's Henry. There's no mistaking that intensity in his eyes. Before I can process what I'm looking at any further, I hear a bone-chilling sound.

A shotgun cocks behind me.

"Put the photo down."

SIX
MORGAN

My eyes flick down to the gun lying at my feet. A bead of sweat travels down my forehead as I contemplate whether I can reach it before the woman behind me pulls the trigger. But before I can reach a decision, I feel the cold touch of steel at the back of my neck.

"Do not even think about it."

I squeeze my eyes shut and draw a shuddering breath. When Catarina said the American who owned this place hadn't been back for years, I'd assumed that meant it was empty. Not that the owner would be Henry, and that he'd left a woman behind.

Who is she to him?

That's the question that brands itself against my every thought. It burns through my blood, drives me to turn and face the woman, staring down the double barrel of a shotgun with my nostrils flaring in anger.

It's the same woman from the photos, and she looks furious. Her lip curls as she snarls and raises the barrel to my forehead, pressing it hard enough to drive me back a couple steps, giving her room to kick the handgun away.

"Who are you?" she asks in an eerily calm voice.

"Morgan," I say. I should be more afraid. After all, I'm staring down the length of a shotgun held by a woman who clearly knows how to use it. But for some reason, I just feel angry. Not at her, but at Henry.

"You are American," she says. It's not a question. If anything, it's a statement tinged with disdain. "Why are you in my house?"

"I didn't think it was yours. I was told it belonged to someone else."

"You are mistaken."

"Am I?" I scoff. I don't know this woman, but I know how rich Henry is. And there's no chance he needed any of this woman's money—if she even has any—to buy it.

"Come with me. I will call the police."

Before she can direct me away, something irrational flares in my chest. My hand shoots out, fingers wrapping around the cool metal of the barrel. She jerks back, startled, but I hold firm.

"Wait." The word comes out sharper than I intended. "Just... wait."

Her eyes narrow, finger still poised over the trigger. "Let go."

But I can't. Not yet. Something about the way she said "my house" doesn't sit right. The certainty in her voice, the territorial anger... it's not the reaction of a housesitter or employee. It's something else entirely.

"How do you know Henry?" I ask.

The question hangs between us like a live wire. Her

grip on the shotgun shifts, and for a moment, I think she might actually pull the trigger. Then something changes in her expression. A flicker of confusion, maybe even vulnerability.

"Henry?" she repeats, his name rolling off her tongue with just the slightest softening of consonants. "How do *you* know Henry?"

I start to open my mouth, ready to share that I am, or *was*, his wife. But something tells me I shouldn't. I don't know if it's the strange look in her eyes, or the simple fact that I've got a gun pointed at me.

So instead, I say, "We were friends."

"Friends?" Her eyes narrow. She doesn't believe me. I don't blame her. Henry was the picture of perfection, well-put together with his tailored suits and neatly combed hair. But me? I don't need to look in a mirror to know I look exactly like what I am now: a second-rate bum who's been living on the streets.

"Yes, friends. I knew him from the States."

"I do not believe you."

"I need you to believe me." The truth slips out before I can stop it.

"What is Henry's last name?" she asks skeptically.

"Langford." I think that's technically my last name now too. I haven't thought about that, really.

"Where is he from?"

"Texas."

She growls and jabs the end of the barrel against me, not liking how easily I'm answering her questions. "You say that you are friends, so answer me this. What does he do when he gets stressed?"

I scoff and shake my head. "He smokes a cigarette."

She stares at me for a moment, her eyes roaming over me with disbelief. I suppose she's probably thinking about how none of my answers had to be exclusive knowledge. I could've probably guessed where he was from. There are only fifty states, after all. And the cigarette thing? Lots of people light cigarettes when they're stressed.

Just then, my stomach rumbles, and we both look down at it. My cheeks flare red with embarrassment.

"You are hungry."

"It seems like it," I say, though I'm honestly starving at this point.

"And you smell terrible."

My cracked fingernails dig into my palms as I look away. "Yeah."

A second passes, then she leans the shotgun against her shoulder. "Meu Deus," she mutters under her breath, shaking her head. "You do not have a home to stay in? That is why you break into mine?"

I don't bother answering. She strikes me as an intelligent woman, with the way I can see thoughts turning behind those brown eyes of hers. She must be able to tell just by looking at me.

The quiet stretches between us for a long moment. Her eyes drift past me to photographs on the mantel, and I follow her gaze to the one of her with the young girl by her side.

"Mama?" A small voice calls from somewhere deeper in the house. "Quem é essa?"

I have no idea what she's saying, but the woman tenses.

"I will kill you if you try anything," she says in a voice so quiet I only just barely catch it.

Light footsteps patter across the marble floors, and then a little girl appears behind the woman. I lock eyes with her as she stares at me curiously, taking in my disheveled appearance. It's the same girl from the photo, just older. And she's even more beautiful in person.

The woman tenses. Though the gun continues to rest on her shoulder, her finger hovers over the trigger, ready to aim and blow me away before I can try anything.

"Sofia, vai para o teu quarto. Agora."

"But Mama, why does the lady look so sad?"

The woman's expression softens momentarily as she looks at her daughter. "Sofia, I told you to go to your room."

"But—"

"Now." The word is final, brooking no argument. The child's face falls, but she obeys, disappearing back into the house with another patter of feet.

The silence stretches between us. She turns back to me, and I see something new in her eyes. My skin prickles.

"That's your daughter," I say quietly. Is she Henry's too? I don't dare speak the thought aloud, even though I'm dying to.

Her mouth forms a thin line. She doesn't say anything. Instead, we just stare at each other, both of us knowing we're dancing around truths neither is ready to share. Truths that we're both desperate to know.

Realizing I'm encroaching on the grounds of a mother with a daughter to protect, I know I have to be the one to break the silence. "So... do you have a name?"

She eyes me, considering me for a moment longer. But then she sighs, moves her finger off the trigger, and nods. "I am Elena."

"It's nice to meet you." I hesitate, then add, "Sorry about breaking in. I thought it was empty."

"You did not know. The women in this city, they gossip about things they know nothing about." She wrinkles her nose. Maybe I smell worse than I thought, because she then says, "You cannot stay in the streets. The police, they will arrest you."

"I know."

"And you say you are Henry's friend." She says it like she's testing the words, seeing how they taste.

"I am."

Something shifts in her expression as she studies my face more carefully, like she's seeing me for the first time. Maybe it's the exhaustion she recognizes, or maybe it's something else entirely. But whatever it is, the immediate danger seems to pass.

Her eyes rake over me with barely concealed disgust. "You need shower very badly. Come."

The way that she says it tells me that I have no option. If you've ever been in another country, you'll know it's not easy to object, not that I would turn down the opportunity for a free shower.

So doing my best not to limp too obviously, I follow Elena through the mansion. We reach a staircase spiraling upward with elegant wrought-iron railings. She leads me to a spacious bathroom, all gleaming marble and brass fixtures, filled with the soft scent of lavender.

Turning toward me with the shotgun still casually resting on her shoulder, she says, "Take a shower. You will feel better. And smell better too."

I should be more wary, but the simple truth is that I'm tired, and I *want* that shower. So I just flash my warmest smile and say, "Thank you."

She studies me with unreadable eyes. "I will bring you clothes. They will fit you."

I glance down at my ragged clothes, my own shame reflected in the pristine mirrors. "Thank you. Again."

Elena doesn't respond immediately, just gives a curt nod and backs out, beginning to close the door behind her. Just before the latch clicks, she pauses and stares at me.

A chill travels down my spine as I lock eyes with her.

Then the door closes.

I wait until her footsteps fade down the hall before I strip out of my clothes, turning the water as hot as I can stand. Dirt, sweat, and anxiety swirl down the drain. I stand beneath the steam, eyes closed, trying not to picture Henry's arm around Elena, laughing on a beach, or the dark-eyed little girl who called Elena "Mama."

I can't help but ask myself... who was Henry Langford, really?

At some point, I hear the bathroom door open and feel the rush of cold air. I freeze, suddenly worrying that Elena lulled me here to pump a shot into me through the shower screen. Bodies are easier to clean up in the bathrooms, right?

But the feeling of cold air disappears a moment later when the door shuts again.

When I emerge, there is a neatly folded stack of clothing set to the side. It's a simple long-sleeved pajama set, but that's all it takes for me to moan in pleasure as I pull on the fresh clothing. I take one look in the mirror and feel so much more like myself.

Following the scent of cooked food, I make my way back downstairs. Elena sits at the kitchen table, shotgun leaned carefully against the wall behind her. A plate of steaming rice, grilled fish, and vegetables awaits me.

"Sit," Elena instructs, motioning toward the empty chair.

I do, cautious as I meet her gaze across the table. She watches me with calculating eyes as I take a bite, savoring the flavor despite myself. The fish is perfectly seasoned with garlic and herbs I've never seen before.

"Better?" she asks.

I nod slowly. "Much."

She crosses her arms, leaning back in her chair with the easy confidence of someone completely in control of their environment. "If you knew Henry, you know he would not want his friend sleeping on the streets."

"You're probably right," I say quietly, testing the word in my head. Friend. I knew that I was supposed to mean something more to Henry, but had I been wrong?

She studies me, then asks. "You need work, sim?"

The offer catches me off guard, and I set my fork down. "What kind of work?"

"Cleaning, laundry, cooking. Help with the house. Nothing too difficult."

I was terrible at all of those things, but I wasn't about to let her know that. It crosses my mind that this might in fact be the worst place to get a job. There's something off about Elena that worries me, but I can't put a finger on it.

"For how long?"

She shrugs one shoulder elegantly. "Until you figure out what you're going to do next. While you decide, you can help me with the house."

I glance toward the hallway, half-expecting the little girl to appear again, but it remains empty. "Is it safer for you, though? You don't even know who I am."

A faint smile flickers at the corners of her lips, but her eyes remain ice-cold. "I am not worried."

A shiver works its way across my skin, and I feel the goosebumps rising.

Elena pushes away from the table, rising smoothly. She picks up the shotgun again, holding it loosely at her side, eyes locking onto mine. "There is a guest room upstairs. First door on the left. Rest tonight. Tomorrow we can discuss this more."

My eyes drift back toward the mantelpiece, to the photo of Henry and Elena, smiling together on that sunlit beach.

My stomach twists.

Something tells me that she was lying about needing help with the house. In fact, it seems like it's in perfectly good shape. There's only one reason she would want me to stay.

She's wondering who I am to Henry too.

And I have a feeling that she won't like the answer I have to give her.

SEVEN
MORGAN

The house settles around me with the kind of silence that wealthy homes have; not truly quiet, but muffled by expensive materials and careful construction. Elena disappeared with Sofia twenty minutes ago.

Now it's just me, alone in a mansion I thought was vacant. If I were smart, I'd probably leave. Catch the first train out of Portugal and forget that I ever came across either Elena or Sofia. That would be the safe thing to do.

But my feet carry me toward the library instead, drawn by those floor-to-ceiling bookshelves I'd glimpsed through the window. The familiar smell of paper and ink hits me as I step inside, and for a moment, I forget everything else.

I trail my fingers along a shelf, spotting the worn spines on older paperbacks, bookmarks still tucked between pages. I see fantasy series with dragons on the covers, thrillers with dark, atmospheric titles that make my librarian heart sing.

Part of me wonders if any of Henry's favorites are here. He'd told me that he read occasionally, but never told me what books he liked. Here, on the shelves, could very well be some of Henry's own choices.

My heart cracks at the thought, a new wave of grief washing over me. How I felt toward Henry was complicated. I can still feel the sting of his betrayal, the way he had completely lied about his relationship with Genevieve. But I can also feel his love, his arms still wrapped around me.

Maybe everything between us wasn't completely fabricated. Maybe some part of what I felt was real.

But then again, standing in the home of someone I fear knew Henry far more intimately than I did, I'm not so sure.

I force myself to leave the library before I can spiral any deeper. There's no point thinking about Henry, or even what this woman's relationship with Henry might be.

I needed to focus on my needs.

The rest of the first floor feels like a museum: beautiful, perfect, and utterly lifeless. Kitchen with granite countertops. Dining room with a table for twelve. Formal living room that looks unused. Everything screams wealth, but nothing screams home.

I'm heading toward the stairs when I notice a door tucked away beneath them. Different from the others. It looks sturdier, with a deadbolt lock that looks newer than the rest of the house's hardware. I try the handle.

Locked.

My pulse quickens. I give the handle another experimental turn, then step back. The voice in my head is screaming now. This is exactly the kind of red flag that should send me running.

Or maybe not. Is a locked door in a house really so strange? I shake my head. My time on that island has made me overly suspicious. I head up to the guest room, exactly where Elena said it would be. It's simple but elegant, with a double bed and ocean view. She left water on the nightstand and towels at the foot of the bed.

I sit down heavily, exhaustion hitting me all at once. My bag slumps beside me, everything I own reduced to stolen clothes and the one thing left from my old life. I reach inside and pull out the diamond ring. Henry's ring, the one he slipped onto my finger during our sham of a wedding ceremony.

It transforms the lamplight into something more like starlight. Beautiful. Expensive. The only proof that, for a brief moment, someone chose me.

I could still sell it. Take the money and disappear completely. Start over somewhere Eden will never think to look. Build a new life with a new name and try to forget Henry Langford ever existed. Forget about this woman and her daughter.

My fingers close around the ring. This is the choice, isn't it? Hold onto the past or let it go. Stay here and torture myself with the truth about Henry, or walk away and never know who or what he really was.

The rational part of my brain is screaming. Leave. Now. Before I get stuck in more trouble than a shower and clean bed is worth.

But the other part—the part that's been starving for answers since I left that island—whispers something different. What if this is your only chance to understand? What if Elena knows something that could give you closure? What if running away means spending the rest of your life wondering if Henry's love was ever real?

I think about Elena's face when I mentioned Henry's name. The flicker of vulnerability beneath her suspicion. And Sofia. That beautiful little girl with Henry's intensity in her gray eyes. Is she his daughter? If she is, then I'm not just walking away from answers. I'm walking away from the only piece of him left in the world.

The thought makes my chest tighten. Because if Sofia *is* Henry's daughter, then Elena might be the only person who truly knew him. Not the version he showed me, but the real Henry.

I stand up abruptly, pacing to the window. The ocean stretches endlessly below, hiding its dark, murky depths beneath all its beauty. Just like everything else in my life. Monsters beneath the surface.

Tomorrow, Elena will want an answer about the job. She'll want to know if I'm staying or going. And despite the fact that trusting people has nearly gotten me killed before, I think I already know what I'm going to tell her.

I might stay and work for the woman who had the thing that neither Genevieve nor I ever had: love enough to bear a child.

God, I think I'm going to be sick.

Why do I love torturing myself like this? I shake my head and climb under the covers, squeezing my eyes shut.

Tomorrow I can make the final decision that'll either give me closure or break what's left of me.

But tonight, for the first time in weeks, I'm clean and fed and safe.

And tomorrow can wait.

EIGHT

MORGAN

The next morning, I'm the first one to wake.

The house is quiet as I rise from bed and shower again. I realize the only thing I have to wear are the pajamas that Elena gave me. But I'm not exactly complaining as I slip them back on. Anything's better than the stained, stinky clothing I had before. I can still smell them from where they're stuffed in the corner of my room.

I head down to the kitchen, morning light streaming through windows that frame the endless ocean. After navigating around the unfamiliar space, I start whipping up breakfast. I've never been much of a cook, but today, I'm all smiles as I enjoy the quiet and the gentle sound of eggs sizzling in the pan.

When they're done, I grab the handle and move to—

"How did you sleep?"

Her voice cuts through the morning quiet, and I catch the suddenly overwhelming scent of her perfume.

The sweet, soft rose layered over a darker undercurrent of musk shocks me with familiarity—I know this smell.

Genevieve.

And for a brief moment in time, when Henry gifted me the perfume... me.

I drop the eggs onto the floor with a loud splat. My smile evaporates as I stare down at the mess, then up at Elena. Her lips are pursed, and her fingers are twitching with barely contained irritation.

"Ah, I'm sorry. You caught me off guard. I'll cl—"

"You will find the mop in the closet behind you," she says in a clipped tone.

Shame floods through me as I fumble for the closet door, my cheeks burning. Of course my first morning here and I'm already making a mess. I can feel Elena's eyes tracking my every movement as I locate the mop and bucket.

I begin mopping up the scattered eggs, trying not to think about how Henry must have given her the same perfume he'd given me and Genevieve. I don't want to think about it, because the more I do, the more it makes me feel like a love-blind fool.

Elena's finger suddenly points in a direction, and following it, I see a spot I missed near the stove. I scramble to clean it, my movements clumsy under her scrutiny.

Uncomfortable in the silence, I clear my throat and speak, going back to her earlier question, "I uh... I slept good. Really good, in fact."

She nods as though it was impossible that it could be

anything other than what she expected. "Good. And my offer?"

"The job?" I pause, wringing out the mop. "Yes, I've thought about it. I'd like to stay and work for you."

Something flickers across Elena's face. Satisfaction, maybe, though it's cold as winter stone. "Muito bem. I expect a high standard of work. You understand this?"

"I would never give you anything less than my best effort. I promise."

She moves past me to a cabinet I hadn't noticed, pulling out cleaning supplies with practiced efficiency. "Working in pajamas will not be accepted."

I glance down at myself and frown. She says it like it's my fault. But not wanting to upset her and risk losing the opportunity to stay and work here, I smile and nod, as though it's a reasonable comment to make to someone who doesn't even own another pair of clothes.

"Do you have any extra clothes that I could wear?"

Elena's expression doesn't change. She walks to another closet and pulls out a neatly folded stack of clothing: a simple black dress with a white apron, the kind of uniform you'd see in old movies about fancy houses.

"You will wear this. Sempre, while working." She hands me the stack, her fingers brushing mine briefly. Her voice carries the weight of absolute authority. "An empregada must look proper, não?"

"Empregada?" I ask. "What does that mean?"

She pauses, looks me in the eye. "It means that you are my maid."

The maid. That's what I am now. Not Henry's wife,

not ever his widow. Just hired help to the mother of his daughter. The irony tastes as bitter as burnt coffee.

I take the uniform, trying to keep my smile in place even as something twists inside me. The fabric is crisp, professional, and completely foreign to anything I've ever worn. "Thank you. This is... perfect."

Elena studies me for a long moment. There's something predatory in how she watches me fold under her expectations, as if my submission feeds some hunger I don't understand. Those dark eyes are unreadable, measuring my willingness to accept whatever terms she sets. And unfortunately, I'm desperate enough to agree to just about anything she says.

Then she nods once, sharp and final. "Get dressed." Elena turns away dismissively, already moving on to other tasks.

As I clutch the uniform to my chest, I catch my reflection in the chrome of the refrigerator. Despite whatever Henry may have thought, I've never been what I would consider beautiful. God knows I'm no Genevieve. But I'm not sure that I've ever looked this rough.

My cheekbones are sharp, my eyes hollowed out, and my hair is thin and falling out. I look like the kind of person who accepts charity from strangers and calls it opportunity.

But is that such a bad thing? For me to find my footing here, among the ghosts of Henry's past?

Maybe.

"Morgan."

I turn at the sound of my name. Elena is standing at the end of the hall, back straight with one eyebrow raised. It strikes me in that moment how gorgeous she is. Here in this house, she seems so elegant and refined. I can tell she grew up around money, much like Genevieve. Henry clearly has a type—other than me, of course. It makes me wonder why he would ever pretend to fall for me.

"You may get dressed in the powder room," she says with a gesture.

I scurry into the small powder room and close the door behind me, rushing to get dressed. The uniform doesn't feel anywhere near as comfortable as the pajamas, its ironed cloth stiff and itchy against my skin. I don't dare look in the mirror because I know I'll be embarrassed by what I see.

Turns out there are much worse things to be than a simple librarian.

When I come out, Elena motions for me to follow her.

She leads me through the house. The click of her heels against marble floors echoes through empty rooms as I hurry to keep up, the stiff fabric of the uniform chafing against my thighs with each step.

"Your day begins at six," she says without turning around, her voice carrying the authority of someone accustomed to being obeyed. "You will prepare breakfast for Sofia and myself. Eggs, toast, fruit. Coffee for me, juice for her. You understand?"

"Yes, of course."

She pauses in the living room, the one with the photographs that had nearly stopped my heart yesterday. In the morning light, the images seem less shocking but no less painful. My heart aches at the sight of Henry's smile.

"Daily tasks," Elena continues, oblivious to my internal spiral. "Kitchen cleaned after each meal. Dishes washed immediately. Floors swept and mopped. Bathrooms and powder rooms—all five of them—cleaned thoroughly. Laundry sorted and started." She turns to face me, those dark eyes assessing. "You have done housework before, sim?"

The honest answer is no. My apartment back home was barely bigger than Elena's powder room, and I'd survived on takeout and paper plates more often than I'd care to admit. But desperation makes liars of us all.

"Yes," I say, hoping I sound more confident than I feel. "I can handle all of that."

"Bom" She moves back toward the kitchen, and I follow closely behind. "Weekly tasks, you must do deeper cleaning. Windows, both inside and out. Baseboards. Light fixtures. The pool area must be maintained." She opens a cabinet to reveal an arsenal of cleaning supplies that would make a professional service jealous. Without help, it's a lot to handle, especially while Henry was off leading a whole other life.

I have a feeling that Genevieve would have murdered him if she'd found out the secret he'd been keeping here: a woman and a child in his house, which by the hour seemed more and more to be *his*.

Shoot, I feel like killing him myself.

"Monthly tasks are more intensive," Elena continues, pulling me from my thoughts. "Deep cleaning of all rooms. Furniture moved, carpets shampooed. Silver polished. Library dusted. *Carefully.*" That last word carries particular weight, as if she knows how much those books mean to someone. Someone like Henry. "The garden requires attention as well. Weeding, pruning, general maintenance."

I nod along, making mental notes while trying not to calculate how impossible this all sounds. I've never managed a pool in my life. I wouldn't know a silver polish from furniture wax. And gardening? The closest I'd come to horticulture was the sad succulent that died on my windowsill after two weeks.

"Groceries and meals are your responsibility," Elena says, opening the massive refrigerator to reveal shelves of expensive, organic everything. "I will provide you with a list of preferred vendors in town. I am particular about Sofia's food. No preservatives, everything fresh. I expect meals planned in advance, ingredients sourced properly."

"Of course. And the budget for—"

"Money is not a concern." She dismisses my question with a wave of her hand. "Quality is. I would rather pay twice the price for half the quantity if it means Sofia eats well."

Another reminder that I'm in a different world now. A world where money flows like water and the only currency that matters is perfection.

"Your day ends at seven," Elena continues, leading me toward the back of the house. "Earlier if all tasks are completed to my satisfaction. You have Sundays free, though emergency situations may require flexibility."

"'That's very generous. Thank you." I don't think she picks up my snarky tone.

She stops abruptly, turning to face me with an expression I can't quite read. "When you go into town for errands, you speak to no one unnecessarily. Purchase what you need and return. The local women, they are... curious about our household. About when Henry will return, why he has been away so long." Her voice takes on a sharp edge. "These conversations are not welcome."

"I understand," I say carefully. "I won't encourage any gossip."

She resumes walking, leading me up the spiral staircase. "This brings me to another matter. Sofia."

We reach the second floor, and Elena's voice drops to something approaching tenderness. It's the first time I've heard her speak with anything other than cool authority.

"My daughter is... how do you say... social. She likes people, likes to talk. But I do not want her becoming too attached to you." Elena pauses at what must be Sofia's room. The door is painted soft pink with hand-painted flowers around the frame. "You are here temporarily, until you find your feet and move on. Yes? It would be cruel to let her believe otherwise."

There's something in her tone that makes my skin crawl. Not malicious, exactly, but cold.

"I understand," I say, though understanding and liking are two very different things. "I'll keep my interactions with Sofia professional."

"Professional," Elena repeats, as if testing the word. "Yes. Professional is good." She moves away from Sofia's door, and I follow her down the hallway. "Your Portuguese is poor, yes?"

Heat rises in my cheeks. "I'm learning. I know some basic words, but—"

"I will speak slowly when needed. Important instructions I will repeat. If you do not understand something, you ask immediately. Mistakes in this house are not acceptable." She stops at the top of the stairs, fixing me with that calculating stare again. "Particularly mistakes that affect Sofia."

The threat is velvet-wrapped but unmistakable. Step out of line, and you're gone. I nod, not trusting my voice to remain steady.

We descend back to the first floor, and I steel myself to ask the question that's been burning in my mind since yesterday. "There's a door downstairs, under the staircase. It was locked. Is that part of my cleaning responsibilities?"

Elena's entire demeanor shifts. The calculated coolness becomes something sharper, more dangerous. She stops walking and turns to face me fully.

"That room is not your concern."

"I just want to make sure I'm not missing anything in my duties and—"

"You are not." Her voice cuts through my words like ice. "It is storage for old things that used to have value. A maid has no business in such places."

But the way she says it, the way her jaw tightens and her eyes narrow, tells me everything I need to know. Whatever's behind that door, it's not old furniture stored away.

"Of course," I say quickly. "I understand."

"Do you?" Elena steps closer, and I catch that perfume again. Genevieve's perfume, the one that connects all three of us in some horrible triangle of shared intimacy. "Because it would be very unfortunate if you misunderstood. Very unfortunate for everyone involved."

The threat is no longer velvet-wrapped. It sits between us like a loaded gun.

"I understand completely," I say, forcing my voice to remain steady. "The locked room is off-limits."

"Bom." Elena's smile returns, but it doesn't reach her eyes. "I think we understand each other very well, Morgan. You need work, I need help. Simple business arrangement, yes?"

"Yes." I agree, though nothing about this feels simple.

Elena glances at an expensive watch on her wrist. "Sofia will be awake soon. You will prepare breakfast. Remember, scrambled eggs for her, and—"

"Coffee and toast for you, right?"

"Yes. After we eat, you begin your first day properly." She moves toward the front door, pausing to collect a purse from a side table. "I have errands in town. I expect the kitchen spotless when I return."

"Where are you going?" The question slips out before I can stop it.

Elena's hand freezes on the door handle. She turns slowly, and for a moment, I think I've overstepped some invisible boundary. But then her expression softens into something that might be amusement.

"I am going to the market to speak with vendors about Sofia's birthday next week. She will be eight." Elena's voice takes on that tenderness again, the mask slipping to reveal genuine love underneath.

"That sounds lovely," I manage.

"Yes. It will be perfect." Elena opens the door, morning light streaming across her face. "Everything in Sofia's life must be perfect. You understand this, yes?"

"Yes."

"I will return in two hours. The kitchen should be clean, breakfast prepared for Sofia when she wakes, and you should be starting on the daily tasks we discussed."

Elena steps outside, then pauses on the threshold. "One more thing, Morgan."

"Yes?"

"The uniform suits you. Very... appropriate." Her smile is full as she adds, "Welcome to your new life."

The door closes behind her with a soft click, leaving me alone in the entryway of a house that feels less like a home and more like a beautiful prison. The grandfather clock in the hallway ticks away the seconds, marking time until Elena's return, until Sofia wakes up, until this strange new existence begins in earnest.

I look down at myself in the black dress and white apron, at the reflection staring back from the polished marble floors. Elena was right. The uniform does suit me. It suits the person I've become: desperate, displaced, willing to accept scraps of kindness from a woman who wears my dead husband's perfume and keeps secrets behind locked doors.

I wonder more and more about that locked door as I head back to the kitchen to start breakfast. But I force myself to push the thought away. I can't ruin a good thing. Not after having seen so much bad.

Everybody's got secrets. God knows I do.

So despite every instinct telling me to run, I search

for the eggs and begin cooking for Sofia. I'll be a maid for a while. Like Elena said, this is just temporary. Eventually I'll get enough saved up to strike out on my own. In the meantime, I can learn more about Henry's past, what Sofia and Elena meant to him, and what *I* meant to him.

It's then that my stomach rumbles.

I never even had the chance to eat.

NINE
HENRY

Today is a good day.

Sure, the word "painful" is insufficient for the agony coursing through every nerve in my body, but it is a *good* day. Of that, I'm certain, because it's the first time I'm standing since the accident.

My body feels like it's being rebuilt from the inside out, muscles and sinew and bones screaming in protest as I stand in front of the mirror. I'm assisted by a mahogany cane topped with sterling silver.

My hand wobbles atop the polished handle, my legs threatening to buckle and send me crashing to the floor. But despite the tremors running through my body, a smile widens across my face.

The doctors are pleased, attributing this incredible rate of recovery to the experimental cocktail they've been pumping through my veins. I know better. It's not some miracle drug that's got me standing again. It's love. Love for Morgan, love for the life we're going to build together, love strong enough to drag me back from the edge of death itself.

I try to take my first step, lifting my foot with concentrated effort. But my foot barely rises an inch before I immediately know it's too soon. My smile disappears in a sudden rush of rage, twisting into an ugly snarl as swear words fly through the air. My eyes land on my cigarette pack, resting on the table across the room. It might as well be on the moon for all the good it does me. I can't even walk there to get it on my own.

The most I can do is simply stand.

Shaking my head, I turn to face the mirror, taking in my appearance. Gone is that handsome, flawless man, and in his place is someone more rugged, scarred across the face and abdomen like a war veteran. Angry red scars line my body where the surgeons had worked their magic. Some people hate scars. I don't mind them, knowing that these were the finest doctors money could buy. If they could've done things without scars, they would have. Which meant that I was a survivor. Which meant that I could *endure*.

So long as I've got Morgan waiting for me, anyway. I need to figure out what I'm going to say to her.

It's strange. Every time I try to think of something meaningful, either the medicine muddles my thoughts into cotton or I'm left speechless. And being speechless simply won't work when I find her. She deserves words, poetry that will let her know that every moment without her has been agony far worse than any physical pain.

I clear my throat and look myself in the eyes. "Morgan, I've missed you more than—" No, that sounds like something from a greeting card.

"Darling, the thought of you kept me alive when—" Too dramatic.

I try again, softer this time. "Morgan, I know you probably think I'm dead, but—" No, no, *no*. Brilliant start, Henry.

Frustrated, I lean more heavily on the cane and attempt something simpler. "Morgan, you're more beautiful than I remembered." Too cheesy. "I never stopped thinking about you." Too desperate. "Marry me again, but for real this time." Too much, too fast.

Dissatisfied with my pathetic attempts at romance, I make a decision that's either brave or spectacularly stupid. I let the cane clatter to the floor.

For a moment—a glorious, terrifying moment—I stand completely unaided. My legs shake like leaves in a hurricane, my vision blurs at the edges, but I'm standing. On my own. Like a man instead of an invalid.

"Morgan, I—"

Then gravity wins, and I collapse backward onto the bed with a grunt that's half pain, half laughter.

The fall should discourage me, should remind me of my limitations. Instead, it fills me with something I haven't felt in weeks: hope. Pure, radiant hope that glows through my chest like sunlight breaking through storm clouds.

I stood. For maybe five seconds, but I stood. And if I can stand today, I can walk tomorrow. And if I can walk tomorrow, I can find Morgan.

It's okay I haven't yet figured out the words. They will come. And when they do...

Everything will be good again.

I stare at the ceiling, ignoring the fresh wave of pain, and let that hope wash over me. Soon—sooner than the doctors think, sooner than anyone expects—I'll be strong enough to leave this place. Strong enough to track down the love of my life and convince her that what we had was real

The medicine might be healing my body, but thinking about Morgan heals everything else.

I can't wait to see her again.

TEN
MORGAN

I've never had so much respect for maids as I do now.

The amount of work involved from dawn until dusk is unfathomable, leaving me dazed through the entire first week. The learning curve associated with each task isn't easy. Making sure there's not even a fingerprint on any of the cleaned dishes, balancing the pool chemicals to precise levels, and the laundry... they required sorting into categories I didn't even know existed.

When I first started cooking for Sofia, I thought I'd be learning more about her, despite Elena's request that I keep my distance. But there simply wasn't enough time. I'd cook, leave her food plated and warmed, and move on to the next task in my endless day.

My body aches in ways I never thought possible. But truth is, even though the work is backbreaking, after staying on the streets, I'm grateful. I have a roof over my head, a bed with actual sheets, and hot water that never runs out. Those are things that a lot of people take for granted. Things I took for granted once, too, until I learned how quickly everything can be stripped away.

Elena watches me work with the intensity of a hawk. She has a talent for appearing silently in doorways when I'm not looking. She'll watch me, point out spots I've missed. It's exhausting, being constantly evaluated and tested and measured against some standard I still don't fully understand.

It's only when the last hours of the day arrive that I find time to unwind. And each and every day, I head to the same place.

The library.

It's soothing in ways words can't describe. The familiar smell of books wraps around me like an old friend's embrace, reminding me of who I used to be before everything fell apart. I guess in a way, this library is my closest tie to home.

My eyes drift across the spines of all the books along the shelves. You could also say that this library is one of my few connections left to Henry as well. I lift my hand and brush my fingers across the spines, walking until a title catches my eye.

I pull it from the shelf. It's a psychological thriller by an author known as Miss Murder. Flipping through the book, I can see it's got short chapters, and judging by the writing style, seems pretty fast-paced. Twisty, too. Just the sort of book that would have been right at home on the recommendation shelf back at the library.

I smile and tuck it under my arm, walking to one of the comfortable leather chairs. I settle in before cracking it open under the warm glow of the table lamp.

I'm three chapters in when I hear the soft patter of bare feet on marble floors. A small face peers around the doorframe, gray eyes wide and curious.

Sofia.

She's been shy around me since that first morning, ducking behind Elena whenever our paths cross, watching me with the careful attention of a child who's learned to be cautious around strangers. But tonight, something's different. Maybe it's the late hour, or the cozy atmosphere of the library, but she steps fully into view.

I smile and motion for her to join me. "Couldn't sleep?"

She nods and pads closer, her pink nightgown decorated with tiny bows. Her dark hair is mussed from her pillow, and she has that soft, sleepy look that all children get when they should be in bed but are too curious to stay there.

"What are you reading?" she asks in careful English.

I glance down at the book in my hands. It's definitely not appropriate for an eight year old.

"A good book, but I'll tell you what," I say gently. "How about we choose a book together, and we can both enjoy it?"

Her face lights up with pure joy, and she hurries over to the children's section. As we browse the lower shelves together, I feel something complex and painful stirring in my chest. Bitterness, because this beautiful little girl might be Henry's daughter. But also something warmer and more desperate. A searching feeling, like I'm looking for some piece of him left in the world.

And I do see it in Sofia. Not just in her gray eyes, but in the way she tilts her head when she's thinking.

She pulls a fairy tale from the shelf; a beautifully illustrated one about a brave princess and a dragon who turns out to be lonely rather than scary. And thankfully, this book is in English instead of Portuguese.

We settle back into the chair together—Sofia curled against my side like she belongs there—and I begin reading aloud, my voice echoing softly in the quiet.

Time passes slowly but peacefully. She asks questions about the pictures, giggles at the funny parts, gasps at the exciting bits. For the first time since arriving in Cascais, I feel... happy.

We're near the end of the story when I notice the figure at the library door.

Elena stands in the doorway, arms crossed, expression unreadable. She's changed into a silk robe, her dark hair loose around her shoulders. I have no idea how long she's been watching us, and my heart lurches as I realize how late it must be. Sofia should have been in bed hours ago, and here I am, directly disobeying Elena's explicit instructions about keeping my distance.

But Elena doesn't look angry. Instead, she has a strange expression on her face that I can't quite decipher. She's watching us like she's studying us.

"Sofia," she says in Portuguese, her voice gentle but firm. "Hora de dormir. Você tem escola amanhã."

Sofia sighs dramatically but slides off my lap without argument. "Boa noite, Morgan," she whispers, then scampers over to her mother.

It takes me a moment to work out what she said.

Good night, Morgan. Elena must have told her to go to bed.

Elena's eyes remain fixed on me as she guides Sofia from the room, and I catch something in her expression that makes my skin prickle. Not anger, but something else entirely. Something that looks almost like approval.

And somehow, that's infinitely more terrifying.

ELEVEN
MORGAN

Funny how I spent my entire childhood studying and earning good grades so I could go to college and get a good job, only to end up on my hands and knees, scrubbing someone else's toilet.

You'd think someone small like Sofia would have smaller poop, but somehow that child has managed to clog the toilet twice this week. I haven't reached the point where I need to mention it to Elena, but if this keeps up, I'll have to broach the topic soon.

In the meantime, I'll probably cut the beans out of her meals. Hopefully that'll make my life easier.

Taking a moment to breathe, I strip off the elbow-length gloves. I wince at the ache in my knees and lower back. Not for the first time, I wish this job were easier on me. But I know what's realistic. This is what it takes to make a living when you don't speak the language and have no transferable skills.

I lean my head against the bathroom vanity, eyes drifting upward to notice that the toilet paper needs replacing. I'd just put in a fresh roll yesterday. It's becoming clear that Elena hasn't done the best job teaching little Sofia proper bathroom habits. But maybe in a house this grand, with past maids presumably handling these issues, there was never any need.

God, to think it wasn't long ago I was sitting on a beach, sipping a passionfruit mocktail.

I shake my head, closing my eyes briefly. When I realize relaxation won't come until I'm done and off this bathroom floor, I pull the latex gloves back on and finish scrubbing.

Five minutes later, the job's done and I'm leaving the bathroom with sweat beading my brow. I glance at the grandfather clock in the hall. It's half past nine. Sofia should be in bed, and I imagine Elena's either in the living room watching television or already asleep herself. Since starting this live-in position, I've realized Elena isn't one for socializing, even with me.

I don't know if it's because I'm the maid, or because we both suspect each other of meaning more to the man we loved. Either way, we haven't talked much.

I can honestly say I know no more about her than I did the day I broke in. Other than the fact that she apparently doesn't know how to teach her daughter to shit right. And I'll say it that crudely because you would too if you'd had to scrub that toilet the way I have.

After a quick shower and change into comfortable pajamas, I head to the library, looking forward to the next book I'd found. Miss Murder's work was excellent, but I'd discovered another that particularly piqued my interest: *Mother, Mother*. So far it's off to a brilliant start.

Except when I arrive at the library, I don't find the peaceful quiet I'd anticipated. Instead, Sofia sits in my chair, waiting expectantly with another fairy tale in her lap.

Seeing me, she flashes a mischievous smile. I don't know if it's because she knows I've just finished scrubbing her mess from the toilet bowl or because she knows she shouldn't be up this late.

"Sofia," I say, raising a brow. "Shouldn't you be in bed? It's a school night."

She lifts a finger to her lips, and God help me, my heart melts at the gesture. The frustration at my disrupted plans fades when she pats the empty space beside her.

Sighing but allowing a soft smile, I cross the library and settle next to her, wrapping an arm around her shoulder.

"Read to me," she whispers.

I nod, take the book from her hands, and begin to read.

Barely half an hour passes before I sense Elena's presence in the doorway. This time I notice.

She stands there watching us, but instead of pausing to acknowledge her, I continue until we finish the story. It ends predictably, with the wicked witch falling into her own cauldron and the rich, handsome prince galloping away on his perfectly white horse with his princess.

I saw the ending coming from miles away, but Sofia didn't. She gasps and looks up at me with wide eyes, then jumps when she realizes Elena is watching. Without a word, she scrambles from my lap and dashes across the library, darting past Elena. We lock eyes and listen to the rapid patter of her feet until we can no longer hear them.

I set the book aside and fold my hands in my lap, resting my head back against the chair. "She's a good kid."

Elena nods. I expect her to turn and go tuck Sofia in or head to bed herself, but instead she crosses the room. She crouches before one of the bookshelves, pulls on a book, and I watch in amazement as a small section slides aside, revealing a hidden wine cooler.

She glances over her shoulder with a devious smile that reminds me of Sofia's. "Gostaria de um copo de vinho tinto?"

I'm not sure what she's said, but I'm guessing she's asking me if I want to drink. That's a risk I'm not willing to take yet, because if I get too vulnerable with Elena... there's no telling what would happen.

"I don't drink," I say.

She shrugs and pours herself a glass, sliding the wine bottle back and closing the hidden compartment. I study the space intently, trying to spot what I'd missed before, but it's impossible. Whoever designed it had exceptional skill and attention to detail. The craftsmanship is flawless; the kind of work that takes both artistry and precision to blend so seamlessly with the existing woodwork.

She settles in the chair across from me and crosses her legs. "Ever since my husband left, my daughter Sofia does not bond easily with people."

A warm feeling bubbles up inside me. It's strange. I hadn't sensed any difficulty bonding from our brief interactions, but sometimes with children you can never tell.

The feeling doesn't last long though. It fizzles away when I process what she said.

Husband.

So that confirms it. Up to this point, I'd been trying to convince myself that she was simply Henry's hidden mistress. He must have married her before Genevieve. Although, I suppose it's possible that he could have married her during their troubles…

After all, didn't he do the same thing to me?

I press my fingers to my temples as a dull throb begins. Questions multiply in my mind. I'm confused, but more than that, I'm furious. So angry that if Henry weren't already dead, I'd bury a knife in his chest and strangle him for good measure.

My eyes drift back to Elena's. She's studying me closely now, that sharp intelligence gleaming. I have no doubt she dropped that word deliberately, and now she's studying my reaction.

I wonder what she thinks of me.

I clear my throat and flash my most sympathetic smile. It's not difficult. I do feel a certain kind of kinship with her. We'd both been women who experienced Henry's warmth, like planets orbiting the sun, only to discover we were never the only ones in his solar system. We'd both basked in what we thought was exclusive light, only to end up burned.

Despite this realization, I'm not ready to share my truth. What if she doesn't feel the same sympathy? She might resent discovering I'd also been married to him. She could kick me out, leave me stranded on Cascais's streets. I'd fall back into ruin, and after finally getting my feet under me again, I don't think I could survive that.

"I'm glad she's able to bond with me," I say quietly in an attempt to distract myself from my thoughts.

Elena nods, her finger trailing around the wine glass rim. She lifts it for a small sip before asking, "Where are you from, Morgan?"

"A place called Des Moines. It's in Iowa."

"That must be quite different from Cascais."

"It is."

"What did you do for a living there?" Her mouth quirks. "I can only assume you were not a maid before."

A slight dig at my housekeeping skills, but I take it in stride. I can't let it bruise my ego given my complete dependence on her. As long as she's keeping this roof over my head, she can say whatever she wants about me.

My finger brushes the book's cover, and for a moment I reminisce about my old life. I lift it with a wistful smile. "I was a librarian."

"A librarian?" She raises an eyebrow. I've caught her off guard. "How different. What brings a librarian from Iowa to Cascais, of all places?"

"A man I once knew said it was his favorite place he'd ever been," I say before I can stop myself.

Her eyes flash briefly. She tucks that detail away, pleased she's gotten something I wasn't ready to share. There's something predatory in the way she does it.

"This man must have meant something to you if you traveled all this way based on that alone." Her tone is deceptively casual, but I can hear the hunger underneath.

Too afraid of what else I might reveal, I don't answer. I just nod.

"I am curious though. You come here, you end up homeless on the street... why do you not just go back?"

I lift my gaze to meet hers. It strikes me how beautiful she is, with her cascade of dark hair and those penetrating brown eyes that seem to see everything. Her bone structure is elegant, refined; the kind of beauty that photographs well and ages gracefully. It's easy to see why Henry might have married her and given her a child.

"Because I can't."

"Oh?"

"I don't have anything waiting for me there."

"But surely your job, your home, calls you back?"

I recognize her probing need to learn more, to uncover the woman who somehow seemed to recognize the man she'd married in her photographs. But how could I ever explain that I, too, was married to him? I wouldn't even know where to begin.

When she sat down tonight, I thought it might be an opportunity to learn more about her. But exhaustion weighs on me. This kind of conversation requires energy I don't have. It's all I can do to fight the pull of sleep right now.

"You know, it's getting late. I should probably head to bed if I want an early start tomorrow."

She studies me longer, her finger continuing to trace the wine glass rim. At first I think she'll object, demand that I stay and explain more about who I am. But instead, she simply says, "Boa noite."

I stand and return the fairy tale to its proper place on

the shelf. My librarian instincts won't let me leave it anywhere but where it belongs. Then I walk to the door and pause.

"It's not that there's nothing waiting for me back there," I say, drawing Elena's attention. "It's just... it's not home anymore."

"And where is home?" she asks.

"Here, I hope," I answer honestly.

At that, she gives me a genuine smile, the first I've seen from her. "Good night, Morgan."

"Good night."

I walk slowly back to my room, the conversation replaying in my mind. The hallway feels longer tonight. Each step echoes softly on the polished floor, a rhythm that matches my heartbeat. When I reach my door, I pause with my hand on the handle, looking back toward the direction of the library where Elena still sits with her wine and her secrets.

I'm sure tomorrow and all the days after will bring more questions, more careful maneuvering around truths neither of us are ready to share. But tonight, for the first time since arriving here, I feel like I might actually be building something: a fragile foundation that could become the home I so desperately need.

I slip into my room and close the door softly behind me, already dreading the morning alarm.

TWELVE
MORGAN

It's amazing how the body adapts when survival depends on it. Three weeks into this strange new life, my hands move through the daily routines without conscious thought. Scrubbing, folding, polishing, I do it all. The muscle memory of servitude has settled into my bones, but the psychological weight of what I'm doing here grows heavier each day.

Part of me wonders what I'm even doing here, working for a woman who was married to what I thought was the love of my life, and taking care of the child they'd had together. It can't be healthy. It must be messing with my subconscious, showing me just how Henry could never have truly loved me the way he loved Elena.

If I ever had any doubt about that, all I had to do was glance at the photos positioned over the fireplace every time I had to dust it. Henry's wide, crinkled smile and the way his gray eyes shone when he looked at Elena, when he looked at infant Sofia.

It's love enough to make me wonder why he ever left

them in the first place. I still don't fully understand the timeline of how everything must have happened, between his ongoing marriage to Genevieve and this marriage or love affair between him and Elena. But I wonder why he wouldn't just leave Genevieve, if he loved Elena this much.

Maybe because he knew that deep down, Genevieve was a psychopath who was capable of murder.

I shake my head and try to turn my mind away from everything. There will be time to peel back the layers of this convoluted onion that is Henry's life. So long as I continue doing a good job for Elena, I can build a life here. I'm even beginning to pick up a few phrases here and there.

The walk into Cascais is becoming more familiar now, my injured leg no longer hurting except on bad days. As I make my way down the cobblestone streets toward the market, I catch the eye of Senhora Martinez, who runs the small bakery on the corner.

"Bom dia, Morgan," she calls out with a warm smile, flour dusting her apron.

"Bom dia," I reply, proud that the Portuguese greeting rolls off my tongue more naturally now. "Como está?"

"Muito bem, obrigada. E você?"

I'm not really sure what she means, but I know the right response from having overheard other conversations. "Bem, obrigada."

The simple exchange fills me with a surprising sense of accomplishment. These small connections feel like tiny victories in a life that's been stripped of almost everything.

I know Elena warned me not to speak to the locals too much, that they liked to gossip and were too curious for their own good. I'm not exactly chatty by nature, so it's not a rule that's particularly difficult to follow. Still, I recognize that I have to interact with people to some degree. After all, if I want to build a life here, then I should have some friends.

Right now, the only person here I could even remotely call a friend was Catarina.

The florist shop sits nestled between a pharmacy and a small grocery store, its windows overflowing with bright blooms that catch the morning light. The elderly man behind the counter speaks broken English mixed with enthusiastic Portuguese, gesturing wildly as he explains the best seeds for Elena's garden.

"Para o jardim, sim? These seeds, muito bom for this soil." He presses packets of lavender, rosemary, and bougainvillea into my hands. "Plant now, before the heat comes. Water every day, not too much, não?"

I nod along, pretending I understand more than I do about gardening. The closest I'd come to horticulture was that sad succulent that died on my windowsill back in Iowa. But Elena expects perfection in all things, so I'll figure it out.

With all the seeds I need in hand, I head back toward the house. But as I pass Café do Horizonte, I spot Catarina through the window, wiping down tables in the afternoon lull. On impulse, I push through the door, the familiar smell of espresso and pastéis de nata washing over me.

"Morgan!" Catarina's face lights up when she sees me,

and she sets down her cloth immediately. "Meu Deus, you look so much better! Healthy, clean, like a real person again."

I laugh, running a self-conscious hand through my hair. "I feel like a real person again. Thank you for everything you did for me before. I don't know what would have happened if you hadn't been so kind."

"Sit, sit," she insists, already moving toward the espresso machine. "Let me make you a bica. It's been too quiet here today."

I settle at a small table by the window, watching the late afternoon light dance across the harbor. The coffee is strong and perfect, warming me from the inside out. For a moment, I almost feel normal, like a woman having coffee with a friend, not an Eden refugee hiding out in some remote country.

"So tell me," Catarina says, settling across from me with her own cup. "What have you been doing? You disappeared for weeks, and now you look..." she gestures at my clean clothes, my healthier appearance. "Like someone took care of you."

"I found work," I answer with a smile. "As a maid, actually. For one of the houses up on the cliffs."

"Ah, good, good." Catarina nods approvingly. "The wealthy Americans, they always need help with their vacation homes. Which house?"

"The white villa, the one you pointed out to me that first day. The one with the infinity pool?"

Catarina's warm smile vanishes, her face draining of color so quickly I think she might faint. "No," she whispers, setting down her coffee cup with shaking hands. "Morgan, no. You cannot work there."

"What? Why?" My heart starts to race at the genuine terror in her voice. "Catarina, what's wrong?"

She glances around the café nervously, as if afraid someone might overhear. When she speaks again, her voice is barely audible.

"That house... it is cursed. There is good reason why its American owner has not returned in many years."

I lean forward, confused. "But I thought you and the other locals didn't like Americans buying up the properties. Isn't that why people avoid those houses?"

"We do not like the practice, sim. But that house..." She shakes her head violently. "That house should be burned to the ground. It brings nothing but death and sorrow to anyone who enters."

"Catarina, you're scaring me. What happened there?"

But she's already standing, her chair scraping against the floor. The fear in her eyes is so raw, so genuine, that my blood turns cold.

"I cannot speak of it. I will not." She looks at me with something like pity. "Morgan, please. Find other work. Anywhere else. That house... it devours people."

"But—"

"I must go." She's already backing toward the kitchen, her movements jerky with panic. "I have... I have things to prepare for dinner service."

"Catarina, wait—"

"Good luck, Morgan. You will need it."

And with that, she disappears into the back of the café, leaving me alone with my cooling coffee and a growing sense of dread that settles in my stomach like lead.

I sit there for several minutes, staring out at the harbor, trying to process what just happened. Catarina's reaction wasn't the typical local resentment toward foreign property owners. This was something deeper, more primal. Pure, undiluted fear.

That house should be burned to the ground.

The words echo in my mind as I finally gather my things and step back into the fading afternoon light. The walk back to the villa feels longer.

As the white walls of the house come into view, gleaming in the golden hour light, I can't shake the image of her pale face, the way her hands trembled when she spoke about the place I now call home.

The house is beautiful, serene and perfect against the cliff's edge and the stretch of ocean beyond. But staring at it, I can't help but wonder... have I stumbled into something far more dangerous than Henry's tangled love life?

THIRTEEN
MORGAN

Today is Wednesday.

My mind's still uneasy with Catarina's warning and the familiar weight of dread sits in my stomach, but I push it down. I can't let paranoia derail the fragile stability I've built here. After all, I can recognize that my sense for danger is probably undermined by the trauma I suffered back on the island.

Besides, I have work to do, because today is Sofia's swimming lesson, and it will be the first time I'm responsible for taking her.

And Elena made it clear that being late wasn't an option.

You'd think that with the beautiful infinity pool here, a swimming instructor would visit the house. But evidently they host the swimming lessons at a community center closer to town, a shared facility that's more central so multiple children can learn together. Elena explained before that it was important Sofia not be so isolated, that she needed to interact with other kids her age.

Elena was good about that, at least—doing her best to make sure Sofia had everything she needed to grow up well. It was one of the few things about her that I genuinely admired, the love and protectiveness she showed toward her daughter.

When I finish planting the last of my garden seeds, I head upstairs and find Sofia in her room, already changed into her bright pink swimsuit with cartoon dolphins scattered across it. She's sitting on her bed, swinging her legs and clutching a small mesh bag containing goggles, a towel, and what looks like a lucky charm: a small plastic starfish.

"Ready for swimming?" I ask, and she nods enthusiastically.

"Will you watch me today?" she asks in her careful English, her gray eyes bright with excitement. "My teacher says I'm really, really good!"

"Of course I will. I can't wait to see what you've learned."

Her face lights up, and she hops off the bed with the boundless energy that only eight-year-olds possess. As we head downstairs, she chatters about her swimming class, her English peppered with Portuguese words when she gets excited.

"There's João, and Maria, and little Tomás who's scared of putting his face in the water. But I'm not scared of anything!" She says proudly. "Papai was the best swimmer, and Mama says I'm just like him."

My steps falter slightly. Papai. Henry. I wonder how much of him she remembers, if he's been gone for so long.

"I'll bet that he was a good swimmer," I manage.

"The best! Mama says he'll teach me when he comes home."

Each innocent mention of Henry's return feels like a knife twisting in my chest. These aren't just Elena's delusions; they're Sofia's hopes, her expectations. What will happen to this little girl when the truth finally comes out?

The walk to the community center takes about twenty minutes, winding down through the narrow cobblestone streets that are becoming familiar to me now. Sofia skips beside me, her swim bag bouncing against her hip, chattering excitedly about her instructor and the other children in her class.

"Professora Ana says I might get to try the diving board!" she says. "But Mama says I have to wait for Papai. He wants to teach me!"

I wonder how many times a day Sofia mentions him, how many plans Elena has made that include a dead man.

The community center is a modest but well-maintained building, all pale stone and large windows that let in plenty of natural light. The pool area buzzes with activity. Children of various ages practicing their strokes while parents and caregivers watch from plastic chairs arranged along the sides.

I help Sofia find her class group and watch as she joins five other children around the shallow end. Her instructor, a patient-looking woman in her thirties, greets Sofia with genuine warmth in rapid Portuguese before switching to slower, simpler words for the benefit of the international children in the group.

I take a seat in one of the plastic chairs and glance at the others. I recognize a few faces from previous trips into town. There's the woman who runs the small grocery store, watching her son practice his breaststroke. A man I've seen at the café sits with a thermos of coffee, occasionally calling out encouragement in what sounds like German.

The familiar sight should be comforting. It's just parents watching their children learn an essential skill. But Catarina's warning keeps echoing in my mind. *That house is cursed.* What does she know about Elena and Sofia that I don't?

"She's a natural swimmer," a voice says beside me.

I turn to find Elena settling gracefully onto the bench, looking effortlessly elegant even in casual white linen pants and a simple blue blouse. Her dark hair is pulled back in a low ponytail, and she's carrying a small leather purse that probably costs more than most people's monthly salary.

"I didn't know you were coming," I say, genuinely surprised.

"I try to make it when I can. Sofia likes to show off when she has an audience." Elena's eyes soften as she watches her daughter slip into the water with easy confidence. "She gets that from her father."

My heart skips at the casual mention of Henry. The way she says it, with such familiarity, such affection, makes it feel like he might walk through the door at any moment. I force my expression to remain neutral, fighting the urge to tell her the truth that would shatter her world.

"He sounds like quite a character."

"He is." Elena's voice carries a wistful note that makes my chest tighten. "He will return soon, I think. It has been too long since he's been home."

He will return soon.

She still believes he's coming back. She doesn't know he's dead, his bones undoubtedly drifting through the ocean since he got shot and fell off the cliff. It's a reunion that will never come.

In the pool, Sofia successfully completes a length of backstrokes, her small arms cutting through the water with surprising grace. She pops up at the far end, water streaming from her dark hair, and waves enthusiastically at us.

"Very good, Sofia!" Elena calls out, clapping. "Show Morgan your butterfly stroke!"

I wave back, managing a smile despite the knot in my stomach. "She's amazing. You must be so proud."

"Every day," Elena says. "She is... how do you say... the light of my life. Everything I do is for her."

There's something fierce in her voice, a protective edge that reminds me this woman held a shotgun to my head just weeks ago. Elena might be showing me her softer side today, but I can't forget that underneath the elegant exterior is someone not afraid of danger.

"How did you and your husband meet?" I ask, desperate to change the subject before my expression gives me away. "You mentioned he'll be coming home soon. You must have quite a love story."

Elena's face lights up with genuine warmth. Maybe the first time I've seen her look truly, unguardedly happy.

"We met at a little café in town called Café do Horizonte. Do you know it?"

My stomach turns as I nod slowly. I suddenly feel like I'm going to throw up. So that's why he loved the café so much.

"I was there with my university friends. He was sitting at a corner table with another woman, reading and smoking, paying her no attention. My friends dared me to go talk to him because he was so handsome. But me, I could see that he was sad."

Another woman? I wonder if it was Genevieve. In any case, I can picture it perfectly. Henry with his intense gray eyes and that restless energy he carried, probably hunched over some thriller novel with an ashtray full of cigarette butts beside his espresso. The image is so vivid, so achingly familiar, that I have to look away.

"And you did? Talk to him?"

"Eventually. It took three visits to the café before I worked up the courage. I had to wait until the other woman was gone." Elena laughs, and the sound is surprisingly genuine, almost girlish. "He was shy too, believe it or not. Kept apologizing for his terrible Portuguese, switching to English every few words. But we talked for hours. About books, about America, about dreams and places we wanted to see."

Her voice trails off, lost in the memory. I watch her face, seeing echoes of the young woman who fell in love with a mysterious American in a coffee shop. It's almost impossible to reconcile this Elena with the one who threatened to kill me if I stepped out of line.

"What kind of books did Henry like?" I ask, genuinely curious.

"Thrillers, mostly. Dark ones about murder and mystery. He said real life was complicated enough. In books, at least the bad guys eventually got caught." Elena's smile turns wry.

The idea of them sitting together, discussing books, shouldn't surprise me. They had a library in their house together. But it does. And it hurts.

"Henry, did he ever tell you much about Cascais?" She asks, studying me so intently it makes me feel like I'm under a microscope.

I scramble for details, drawing on the few things Henry had actually told me about Portugal during our brief time together.

"Mostly just that it felt like home to him. Something about the pace of life being different, more authentic than the States. And something about the cigarettes being cheaper here than in Texas." I manage a small laugh.

Elena nods, seemingly satisfied. "Terrible habit. I kept trying to get him to quit, especially after Sofia was born, but..." She shrugs. "Some battles you cannot win. He promised to quit when he returned. Said fatherhood would give him the motivation he needed."

The casual mention of promises he'll never be able to keep makes my throat tight. Elena has built her entire future around words from a dead man.

In an attempt to mislead her, I ask, "Do you still talk to him? While he's away, I mean?"

Elena's expression grows sad, almost vulnerable again. "Distance is difficult, Morgan. We do not speak as much as I would like."

Yeah, I'm not surprised. He's dead. And married, twice over. Asshole.

The sound of her voice is heartbreaking. She's been waiting for a dead man, raising his daughter alone, keeping his house perfect for a return that will never come. And she has no idea that the love of her life died thinking about someone else entirely. God, what would she do to me if she knew he died when we were about to exchange our final vows?

"How long has it been since you've seen him?" I ask softly, hoping it might give me some idea of the extent of his cheating.

"Too long." Elena's fingers twist in her lap, the only sign of her distress. "Sofia needs her father. And I... I miss him. Sometimes I wake up and forget he's not there. I reach for him in bed, and find only empty space."

The raw honesty in her admission catches me off guard. For a moment, she's not the calculating woman who controls every aspect of my daily life. She's just a mother and a wife, missing the man she loves with an ache that's almost palpable.

Despite everything, I feel a stab of genuine sympathy for her. We're both women who've loved Henry Langford. We're both paying the price for that love in different ways, though she doesn't know it yet.

"I'm sure he misses you too," I say, and I mean it. Whatever else Henry was, whatever lies he told, the love in those photographs was real. The way he looked at

Elena, at baby Sofia... that wasn't something you could fake.

Elena turns to look at me, and for a moment, something passes between us. An understanding, maybe. Or just the recognition of shared pain that transcends our complicated situation.

"Obrigada," she says quietly. "Thank you. It's... it's nice to talk to someone who knew him. Even a little. Sometimes I worry that I'm keeping his memory too alive for Sofia, that I should let her forget and move on. But how do you forget love like that?"

The question hangs in the air between us, heavy with implications. How *do* you forget love like that? I'm still trying to figure out the answer myself.

In the pool, Sofia has moved on to practicing her butterfly stroke, her small body moving through the water with determined concentration. Other children splash around her, but she's focused on perfecting her technique, probably wanting to show off for us.

"She has his determination," Elena observes, watching her daughter. "When Henry set his mind to something, nothing could stop him. Sofia is the same way."

"It's a good quality to have."

"Yes, but also dangerous. Determination without wisdom can lead to... difficult choices." Elena's voice carries a weight that makes me look at her, but her expression is unreadable.

We sit in comfortable silence after that, watching Sofia practice her strokes. The afternoon light streams through the large windows, casting rippling patterns on the pool's surface. The sounds of children laughing and splashing create a peaceful backdrop, and for a few minutes, I almost forget about the complexities that brought me here.

But then Elena speaks again, her voice carefully casual.

"You said you lost touch with Henry. When was the last time you saw him?"

The question feels like a trap, and I choose my words carefully.

"It's been a few years. Like I said, we weren't close friends, just acquaintances. I probably wouldn't even recognize him now if I saw him. People change, you know?"

"Not Henry," Elena says with absolute certainty. "He doesn't change. The same laugh, the same way of running his hand through his hair when he's thinking. The same gray eyes that see everything." She pauses. "I would know him anywhere."

The conviction in her voice sends a chill down my spine. What will happen when Elena finally accepts that Henry isn't coming home? What will she do with all that love when it has nowhere to go?

The swimming lesson ends, and Sofia comes running over to us, dripping wet and beaming with pride.

"Did you see my butterfly? Professora Ana says I'm the best in the class!" She wraps her small arms around me, getting me soaked in the process.

"I saw, minha querida," Elena says from the side. "You were magnificent. Papai will be so proud when he sees how much you've improved."

"Will you tell him? When he calls next time?" Sofia asks eagerly.

"Of course, meu amor. Every detail."

I watch her, realizing she must tell Sofia that they speak on the phone occasionally. After all, how do you tell your daughter you haven't spoken in years?

As we walk home together afterward, Sofia skipping between us and chattering about her swimming progress, I can't shake the image of Elena on a phone call, talking to empty air and maintaining the fiction that Henry is still out there somewhere, still coming home.

The sun is setting by the time we reach the villa, painting the white walls golden in the dying light. Beautiful and serene, just like always. But now I can't help wondering if Catarina was right. Maybe some houses really are cursed.

Maybe some secrets are too dark to ever see the light.

And maybe some love is too dangerous to ever survive the truth.

FOURTEEN
HENRY

My heart is pounding.

It's *been* pounding since I stepped off the plane, because I know that the moment I go through those doors, I will see her. My beautiful wife, who I thought I would never see again.

I still haven't managed to figure out exactly what I want to say. The essence of it all, that part I know. But the *words* continue to evade me.

I lift a hand from my mahogany cane to my heart, feeling it race inside my chest, willing it to calm just enough for me to catch my breath. I tell myself that when the moment comes, I will know what to say.

After all, this is exactly how I'd felt the moment I first saw her. Those green, luminous eyes staring back at me, the soft curve of her lips and the delicate line of her throat. From that moment to now, she has been mine, just as I have been hers and only hers.

I lift my chin, draw a deep breath, and remind myself: She wants me, she needs me, she loves me.

The words I say will be important in the moment, but only ever in this moment. What we'll remember walking away from this is that I came back from the dead for her, and that never again will we have to spend a night apart.

Not with Genevieve out of the way.

I take a step forward, the sound of my accompanying cane tapping alongside every footstep. I feel the tides of fate carrying me along. The people nearby part to the side like the Red Sea, and when I reach the door, someone presses the handicapped button on the wall, making it open of its own accord.

The silence of the library embraces me.

I have to admit, I never thought I would be paying a visit to Des Moines. Morgan had been clear from the start that there wasn't much for her here. But ever since my fall from the cliff, I've known she would come back here. It's how the human mind works. When crisis hits, we seek out the things we know.

I step inside, my gaze immediately swinging to the front desk where two librarians are stationed. It takes me longer than I'd like to cross the hall to them, especially as the tap of my cane announces my presence and has them facing me before I'm even close.

An awkward moment settles into the silence around us as I slowly approach.

"Hello, how may we help you?" one of them asks.

I peer from side to side, searching for some sign that my wife is here. But when I see none, I frown. "I'm looking for my wife."

"Your wife?" one asks. She exchanges a look with the other librarian. "What's her name? If it's an emergency,

I'd be happy to make an overhead announcement for her to come to the front desk."

I shake my head. "My wife actually works here, you see."

The two librarians exchange another look. "Are you sure?"

"I am positive."

The other woman steps forward. "What's her name?"

"Morgan Sloane." I hesitate, then add, "Morgan Sloane-Langford."

"Morgan?" The woman's brow furrows, then her eyes light up in recognition. "Hang on... you're the guy she married at first sight? From that Eden program?"

My eyes dart around nervously to check if anyone's listening. Thankfully, everyone else seems engrossed in their books. The last thing I need is more people looking into Eden and getting themselves into the same heap of trouble Morgan and I got into.

"Look," I pause and check her name tag. "Tiana. I just need to know if she's here or not."

The other woman comments, "Damn, Tia, if there are men like this signing up to get married at first sight, maybe I should consider it."

Tiana's eyes are wide and she quietly nods. It's clear that I'm not what she or her friend were expecting when they gossiped about the crazy coworker who dashed off to marry a man she'd never met.

"Don't," my voice snaps.

The woman flinches, her smile fading. Maybe my tone was too harsh, but better that than her discovering the truth about the program. I should never have let

Genevieve convince me to do it. Well, no, I take that back. If I hadn't signed up for Eden therapy, I never would have met the love of my life.

"If Morgan's not here, do you know where she has gone?" I ask, turning back to Tiana.

"I haven't seen her since she left to get married to you." She pauses. "You don't know where she is?"

"We... had an argument. I'm trying to make it right."

The other woman starts to smile. "How romantic."

I have a feeling she'll be looking into Eden the moment she gets home. But that's not my concern. My one and only concern in this life is my wife.

Tiana considers me, then shakes her head. "I don't think I can help you."

My breathing slows. Have I been mistaken about her returning here? "Please. Think real hard. You don't know where she might be?"

"No idea. We weren't that close."

"She never talked about any other places she wanted to visit?"

"Never."

I rake my hands through my hair before reaching into my pocket for my pack of cigarettes. I'm really not supposed to smoke yet, according to the doctors. But I can't fight the urge right now. It's either this or let the anxiety and worry eat me whole. Better to smoke it all away so I have a clear mind to figure out where Morgan could have possibly gone.

Just as I'm about to light the tip, Tiana purses her lips and says, "There's no smoking in here."

My thumb freezes over the lighter, my eyes flicking

up to meet hers. She's a difficult one, I can tell that much. But still, this is her library, and I need to respect it. I put away the cigarette and smile. "Thanks for the help."

I stab my cane into the ground as I pivot and start to leave.

"Hey, wait! What's your name?"

I don't bother answering as I leave. If she wants to know who I am, she can simply google my Langford name. That'll tell her everything she needs to know, except for the one thing that matters—that I'm head over heels in love with Morgan Sloane.

The afternoon air hits me as I emerge from the library's climate-controlled sanctuary. Iowa in summer is nothing like the sophisticated comfort of the Eden resort. It's humid and thick, the kind of air that clings to your skin and makes you feel trapped.

Much like how I feel right now.

I lean heavily on my cane, the reality of the situation beginning to settle over me. She's not here. Morgan—my brilliant, beautiful, complicated wife—is not in the one place I was certain she would be.

My legs are already aching from the short walk through the library, but I force myself to move toward a nearby bench. The pain medication makes everything fuzzy around the edges, but it can't dull the sharp panic beginning to claw at my chest.

Where could she be?

I pull out my phone and scroll through my contacts, though I'm not sure who I could possibly call. Morgan doesn't have family. She'd been painfully clear about that during our conversations on the island. No siblings, no extended relatives who might take her in. Her parents were dead, and from what I gathered, she'd been essentially alone in the world even before Eden found her. It's not surprising that Eden selected her out of all their applicants. She was the perfect candidate to be a stand-in wife they could easily get rid of.

I shake my head and continue thinking through where she could be. The apartment she lived in is obviously out of the question. My driver drove past it on the way to the library, only for us to see a "For Rent" sign in the yard.

She's running. She has to be. After everything that happened on the island, she must think that she's being hunted. She'd want to disappear completely, go somewhere that Eden would never think to look.

I still can't shake the simple fact that human psychology isn't so easy to escape. She *would* seek out someplace of comfort.

But where?

I close my eyes and try to think like her. If she thought she was being hunted, she wouldn't go somewhere obvious, wouldn't leave a trail that could be followed. She'd choose a place that meant something to her but that she'd never mentioned to anyone else.

Except...

My eyes snap open, heart suddenly racing for an entirely different reason.

There was one place. One location I'd mentioned to her during those long conversations over our romantic dinners. I'd been talking about travel, about places that had changed me, and I'd let slip about a little coastal town in Portugal that had captured my heart years ago.

Cascais.

I can't explain how I know it, but the moment I think of Cascais, I know she's there. Morgan isn't just running. She's running to the one place on earth she knows I loved. She's searching for some way to feel close to me even though I'm supposed to be dead.

A smile spreads across my face, slow and certain and probably slightly manic from the pain medication. But I don't care.

She went to Cascais.

And that can only mean one thing.

She loves me. Truly, desperately, *completely* loves me.

Just like I love her.

I push myself up from the bench, ignoring the sharp protest from my still-healing body. My cane taps against the sidewalk as I head toward the car.

My driver opens my door, and as I get in, I say, "Have the plane ready. We're headed to Portugal."

"Yes, sir."

The door slams shut behind me. I have to admit, when I walked out of the library, I felt hopeless. Now, I feel as light as a feather, because I know exactly where my wife is waiting for me.

FIFTEEN
MORGAN

Life is beginning to get better.

Hard but better. Every day is filled with strenuous work that leaves me exhausted in ways I've never experienced, but I have to admit that when the day comes to a close and I'm sitting in my chair in the library, I feel... content. There's a satisfaction that comes from honest labor, a sense of purpose I never found shelving books or helping readers find the latest and hottest romance novels. It's the kind of achievement that can only be earned through sweat and dedication, through proving to yourself that you can survive anything.

I'm still curious about Elena and Sofia, but after my talk with Elena at the pool, I've decided that maybe I don't need to know the truth. After all, I know enough. Henry loved Elena, and the reasons why are clear.

She's intelligent, beautiful, and despite her cool exterior, she has a warm heart. We haven't talked much since that day at the pool, but I think she's starting to warm up to me. She's smiling more around the house, dressing more relaxed, though still quite put together, much like Genevieve used to be.

Occasionally, I'll still catch her watching me, studying me, like she's trying to figure out the truth about me. But I don't plan to ever tell her. Eventually, she'll learn that maybe she knows enough too.

"Morgan!" Sofia's voice carries from ahead, and I lift my gaze. The corners of my eyes crinkle as I watch her skip backwards, smiling and waving toward me. "Vamos! Come on!"

It seems her favorite cartoon, *Ruca*, is supposed to come on soon, and today is supposed to be a particularly good episode.

"I'm coming, I'm coming," I say, limping my way up the garden path. Most days my leg doesn't bother me, but today isn't one of those days.

"Hurry up, Tia Morgan!"

I stumble over a step. Sofia doesn't seem to realize what she's said as she turns and runs toward the house. But her voice plays over and over in my mind. *Tia Morgan.* Auntie Morgan. My heart flutters before warmth spreads throughout my body.

I had always envisioned having children with the perfect husband; a house full of laughter, bedtime stories, scraped knees to kiss better. But ever since arriving in Cascais, I've had to accept some dreams might remain forever out of reach. Maybe this borrowed family, this borrowed life, is as close as I'll ever get to that white-picket-fence fantasy of mine.

I watch Sofia ahead as she reaches the door, her dark hair bouncing with each enthusiastic step, and I can't help the smile that spreads across my face. In her innocent world, I'm not the maid, the intruder, or Henry's secret wife. I'm just the woman who reads her stories and makes her lunch.

Tia Morgan.

I think I can get used to being called that.

The pain in my leg fades against the backdrop of happiness, and I reach the house. I fit the key into the lock and push the door open, chuckling to myself as Sofia darts inside and flies toward the family room where the television lives: a cozy space off the main living area with comfortable sofas and walls lined with Sofia's artwork. Soon, the cheerful sounds of her cartoon echo down the hallway.

I head to the kitchen, which gleams like something from a magazine spread thanks to my early morning efforts. Every surface sparkles, the marble countertops are spotless, and even the inside of the microwave has been scrubbed clean. It's amazing what you can accomplish when you start at six in the morning.

Humming to myself, I withdraw a pan and set it on the stove. I light the burner and start preparing something simple: grilled cheese and tomato soup, comfort food that reminds me of winter afternoons in Iowa when the snow piled high against the library windows. Something from home, even if home feels like a lifetime ago.

I finish cooking and carry the tray upstairs to the family room, where Sofia is curled up on the sofa, completely absorbed in her show. I set the food on the coffee table beside her.

"Obrigada, Tia Morgan!" she says without taking her eyes off the screen.

"De nada," I reply, surprised by how naturally the Portuguese response comes. I'd never believed it, but being immersed in another culture really is the best way to learn a new language.

Back in the kitchen, I'm just finishing the cleanup when I hear the front door open and close. The telltale sound of Elena's heels against the polished stone floors tells me it's her, and sure enough, she appears in the doorway a few moments later.

"Good timing," I say. "I've just finished a late lunch for Sofia. Want me to make you something?"

I cross my fingers that, like most days, she's already eaten. The garden has been weeded, the floors mopped throughout the house, and the bathrooms scrubbed. With all that work done, I have nothing else on my schedule for the day, which means I could make it to the library early and maybe even finish *Mother, Mother*—I'm completely hooked and dying to know how it ends.

But instead of declining my offer, she flashes me a smile with a strange look in her eye. "That would be wonderful. I did not have lunch because of my meeting."

I've overheard enough phone calls now to know that Elena runs some sort of online business. Something to do with reselling high-end vintage clothing. I don't really know, but it seems to be doing well enough that money never appears to be a concern. Though I suppose it's possible the business is a money pit and she's surviving off a bottomless account Henry set up for her.

I draw a sharp breath, a wave of disappointment

washing through me. But I force a smile and nod, giving the pan a quick wash in case she wants the same thing I made Sofia.

"Is there anything in particular you want, or would you like grilled cheese and tomato soup too?" I ask.

Elena takes a seat at the kitchen island and taps a finger against her chin, like she's thinking. But she's still got that strange look in her eye. Her smile grows wider. "Do you know how to make bacalhau à brás?"

I grimace. "I... don't. But I can look it up if you like?"

She shakes her head. "No need. I will show you how to make it."

Before I can object, she ties her dark hair back into a bun and rounds the island. She motions for me to stand beside her as she starts to gather ingredients: salted cod, potatoes, eggs, onions, olive oil, and fresh parsley.

"First, we must soak the bacalhau," she explains, her voice taking on the patient tone of a teacher. "The salt, it must come out slowly. Then we shred it, very fine, like this." She demonstrates with her hands, showing me the proper motion. "The potatoes, we cut into thin strips and fry them until golden."

I nod along, but in all honesty, everything she's doing is going over my head. I'll definitely look this up later... if I can remember what the dish is even called.

"Now the onions," she continues, heating olive oil in a large pan. "We cook them until they are soft." The onions sizzle as they hit the hot oil, filling the kitchen with the sweet smell. "You see?"

"Uh... yeah, I do," I lie as I try to play back everything she did.

"Do you ever miss Henry?"

The sudden question catches me off guard. I clear my throat, my mouth suddenly dry. "Miss him? I mean, I don't know that I really knew him well enough to miss him. We were just friends."

Was that a lie or the truth? I'm not sure. We'd only just met, gotten married, and started exploring each other. And then, before I even had a chance to learn as much as I'd hoped, it was all over. Maybe that's a good thing. With Elena and Sofia... it seemed like I knew more lies than truth.

Still, it doesn't ease the ache in my chest.

"So you never kissed him?" she asks in a deceptively calm voice that thickens the air with tension.

"No. I never did." I can still picture his face as he leaned in—the stubble of his beard, his flawless skin, his impossibly long eyelashes. It was a strange detail to fixate on, but it was always the last thing I saw before I closed my eyes and met his kiss. I can still taste his lips, even now.

My hands tremble and I clasp them together to keep them from shaking where Elena might notice.

Elena doesn't say anything, doesn't comment or even so much as glance my way. Instead, her voice drops to a whisper, and she asks, "So you never had sex?"

My tongue darts across my lips as a sudden wave of nervousness crashes over me.

"Never felt his hands on your body?" she presses, her tone growing more insistent.

I hesitate a second too long before the word finally crosses my lips. "No. Where is this coming from?"

She stops. Turns to face me. One hand still grips the pan handle. Her dark eyes bore into mine, and slowly, the smell of burnt onions begins to fill the air.

I stare back, unwilling to budge or say anything. Partly because I know that anything I say would only make me seem more guilty. And partly because I'm afraid she'll take that hot pan and smash it against the side of my skull.

"You never felt the desire to do so?" she asks.

This time, I don't hesitate. "No."

Her sharp gaze lingers on me for a moment longer, until she finally nods and looks away. She doesn't pay me any attention as she continues cooking the dish like it isn't burnt. "I would not blame you if you did have the desire. He was a handsome man. A very... desirable man. Any woman should feel so lucky as to have him."

She definitely suspects something about my relationship with Henry. But does she have any clue what Henry had with Genevieve? I'm not sure. The thought of what she might do if she found out makes my stomach twist. I can still see that deadly look in her eyes from when she first caught me in this house, shotgun pointed at my head, finger hovering over the trigger like she was deciding whether I was worth the cleanup.

Damn it, Henry. Why did you have to be such a piece of trash? Not only did you put me through some twisted fake marriage while trying to save your real marriage, but you never mentioned the *second* wife you had here, in your favorite place in the world.

Never trust men. They're not worth the effort it takes to divorce or bury them.

I swallow and smile. "Henry was good looking, sure, but he's not my type."

She raises a brow. "Really?"

I smile and nod, not trusting myself to explain why. Because the truth is Henry was *very* much my type. From his personality and interests to his movie-star good looks, he was everything I'd ever dreamed of finding. Except for the one quality that matters most in a spouse. *Honesty*.

Elena seems to accept this, or at least pretends to. She turns back to the dish, scraping away the burnt onions while continuing to teach me the proper technique. The bacalhau comes together beautifully despite the mishap: golden potatoes, flaky cod, and perfectly scrambled eggs all folding together in the pan.

"You see? Even when things burn, they can be saved with a little patience," she says, plating the dish with practiced elegance.

I nod, though I'm not sure we're still talking about food.

"I should check on Sofia," I say, backing toward the doorway. "Make sure she's not getting into trouble."

Elena waves me away with a dismissive gesture, but as I walk down the hallway, I can feel her eyes burning into my back.

SIXTEEN
MORGAN

"Morgan."

Henry's voice slices through the darkness like broken glass. It jolts me awake into a strange space where nothing exists but his voice and the weight of my consciousness floating through emptiness.

"Henry?" I call out, spinning around. But there's only darkness stretching in every direction.

Then I feel his hand on my shoulder, and I know it's him. I look over to find his beautiful gray eyes staring back at me. His mouth curves into that smile I remember, and before I can think, he pulls me against him.

He's everywhere—his scent, his warmth, the solid feel of him. God help me, that jagged crack in my heart starts to heal. Everything's going to be okay. We're exactly where we're supposed to be, except...

Elena.

I can feel her lurking somewhere nearby, watching me like she always does. All the warmth drains out of me, *replaced by the chill of her presence. And I don't want her seeing this.*

I try to pull away, but Henry's arms lock around me.

"Henry," I whisper, terrified Elena might hear me even now.

"What is it, my love?"

"Do you see her?"

"Who?"

I frown and try to step back, but his grip tightens. His fingers press into my ribs, hard enough to bruise. Hard enough to hurt.

"Henry!" I gasp, and when I say his name, he squeezes harder. "Stop. You're hurting me."

He doesn't listen. Or maybe he doesn't care. His arms keep tightening.

"Please! Let go!"

Then suddenly he releases me, and I stumble backward, wrapping my arms around myself as I fight to catch my breath. My ribs throb where his fingers dug in. I stare at him, but the darkness is creeping closer, seeping into everything until I can barely think straight.

Because when I look up, Henry's gone.

And Elena is standing in his place.

She wants me dead. I can see it in her eyes. She steps forward, and I step back. She takes another, and I'm scrambling, knowing what she's capable of. If I had a daughter and some woman had lied to me about my husband, I'd want her dead too.

"Elena, this isn't what it looks like."

"Do not lie."

"Elena!"

Fingers tangle in my hair from behind and yank my head back. I try to see who's grabbed me, and it's Henry again. But something's wrong now. His face twisted into something ugly and cruel. Those gray eyes I once loved burn with hatred.

"You actually thought you mattered?" His voice sounds different now. There's nothing left of the kindness I knew. "You were only ever a tool for me, Morgan. Something to use and throw away. That's all you've ever been."

Elena watches with cold satisfaction, like she's enjoying every second of this.

He drifts past me through the void toward Elena, and she never takes her eyes off me. Her smirk widens as she reaches up and lets her hair tumble down over her shoulder. Her fingers find the straps of her dress and ease them down, one after the other.

Some invisible force holds me captive, forcing me to watch as her naked body presses against Henry's. Her legs wrap around his, then his waist as he lifts her up. I can't even close my eyes as he takes her with a passion so raw and desperate that every last doubt about who Henry really loved gets burned away. This is what real desire looks like. What I thought we had was nothing compared to this.

Maybe this is how Genevieve felt, watching through that window as Henry and I made love in those final days on the island. Maybe this helpless rage is exactly what drove her to pull that trigger.

A scream builds inside me, clawing at my throat, but even that is trapped in this nightmare. Pain shoots through my stomach, surging up into my chest and neck. The scream grows and grows until it finally erupts, shattering the darkness and their writhing bodies into a thousand pieces.

I jolt awake, soaked in sweat with my blankets twisted around my legs. I look down and see angry red scratches covering my body. I've clawed myself half to death in my sleep. They're not bleeding yet, but they'll take days to heal.

I collapse back against my pillow, kicking off the covers and letting the cool air wash over my skin. Maybe this was a mistake, trying to build a life in the wreckage Henry left behind. Trying to build a foundation on his wife—ex-wife? I don't even know—and his daughter.

It's pretty sick when you think about it. If I was in Elena's shoes and suspected the truth, I doubt I'd be so graceful about it.

I lie there staring at the ceiling, but slowly that familiar prickle creeps across my skin. The feeling of being watched. I scan the room but see nothing. Then I notice the door. It's cracked open just enough for someone to peer through.

I stare at that sliver of darkness, and my chest tightens. Something's there. A shadow, a silhouette that looks like...

The blackness shifts just enough to make my skin crawl.

I throw off the covers and cross the room quickly, yanking the door open. But the hallway is empty.

Nothing but moonlight streaming through the window at the far end.

I sigh and head to the bathroom, splashing cold water on my face before staring at myself in the mirror. It's strange how I look the same but feel completely different. I'm not the naive woman who went to that island looking for love. I found it, all right, and it burned me.

The door creaks.

My eyes snap toward the sound, and my hand closes around my toothbrush. It's the closest thing I can grab, and flipped around, it could make a decent weapon. I think if I stabbed hard enough into something soft—an eye, maybe, or the throat—it could do some real damage.

I peer out of the bathroom, armed with my makeshift weapon as I scan the room. "Hello?"

Nothing. The silence swallows everything just like before. Part of me wants to retreat back into the bathroom and lock the door until sunrise. But I'm not going to do that. That's what the old Morgan would have done.

I step into the bedroom and move toward the door, my bare feet silent on the cold floor. I stick my head out into the hallway and let my eyes cut through the darkness, but I still don't see anyone.

Frowning, I step back and close the door firmly behind me. I drag my hand down my face. Maybe I'm losing it. Between the nightmare and whatever game Elena's playing, I'm starting to crack. Sleep deprivation does things to your mind. Makes you see and hear things where there aren't any. I learned that the hard way during those first nights on the streets.

I turn back toward my bed and freeze.

There's a lump under the covers that wasn't there before. I'm the kind of person who sleeps with exactly one pillow, and this is something else entirely. The sheets are disturbed, and worse, they're moving up and down like something's breathing underneath them.

I raise the toothbrush overhead and yank the covers back.

Sofia's face stares up at me. I let out an explosive breath, my whole body sagging with relief.

"Sofia, what are you doing here?"

She scrunches up her face tiredly. "I couldn't sleep. I wanted to sleep with you."

I shake my head. "You can't stay here. You need to go back to your own bed, or your mother will be very unhappy."

"Please?" She gives me those big gray eyes—Henry's eyes—and my resolve starts to crumble. "I had a scary dream."

"Sofia..."

"Please, Tia Morgan? Just tonight?"

How can I say no to that face?

I sigh and climb into bed beside her. She immediately cuddles up against my side, her small body warm and trusting. It feels... nice. Better than nice, actually. Like maybe I need this more than she does. Maybe having her here will keep the nightmares away.

In some twisted way, it almost feels like I'm holding onto a piece of Henry. Even though I'm growing to hate him the more I learn the truth, I can't let that affect Sofia. She's innocent, and seemingly has all the best parts of him.

So as my eyes close, I allow myself to dream of another place, another reality. One where she doesn't belong to Elena, but to me. One where Henry wasn't dead, and didn't deserve his death.

One where I could be happy.

SEVENTEEN
MORGAN

"What are you doing?"

The cold voice snaps me out of sleep. I gasp as I jolt awake, taking in everything all at once: the little girl still asleep in my arms, my covers pulled up over us both, and Elena standing over me, her shadow no darker than the look on her face.

I pale and quickly untangle myself from Sofia, who does nothing but scrunch up her face and turn the other way. It can't be that bad, getting caught with Sofia, right? It's innocent, and Elena's heard her call me Tia Morgan. It can't be...

Oh, no.

It's a school day. What time is it? A single glance at the clock tells me she's late, and worse, I was supposed to be the one to take her.

I turn guiltily toward Elena, unable to keep the grimace from my face. I hold up my hands. "Elena, I—"

Her lip curls and she holds up a hand, stopping me

mid-sentence. "Sofia!" Her voice echoes loudly against the heart-stopping backdrop of silence.

Sofia looks back over her shoulder and frowns. "Sim, Mama?"

"Head to your room. Get dressed. You're late for school."

Sofia's gaze swings to me, then back to her mother. I know she must be too young to understand the significance of the trouble I'm in, how this could undo me entirely. There's no way she can know that I'm going to be thrown back out onto the street, and that it's there I'll likely get caught and sent to prison. But she's old enough to know that I'm in trouble.

She pushes back the covers and, moving at a snail's pace, slinks out of the room.

I turn to Elena, but before I can speak, she silences me with a glare.

"You Americans are too bold. Do you think it appropriate for me to come in here and find my daughter sleeping in your arms?"

I stutter as I try to answer, "I know. I... look, I know it's not great. But it's okay, right? Me and Sofia—"

Her brow lifts, her mouth parts in disbelief. "You think this is okay?"

"I wasn't doing anything to her. She came to me and got in my bed, not the other way around."

Her look of disbelief transforms into something colder, more calculating. She crosses her arms and tilts her head slightly, studying me like I'm a specimen under glass. "You think that I assume something... malicious is going on here?"

I blink, suddenly unsure of where this is heading. "Don't you?"

"I do not. I know that you would never do anything untoward with my daughter. Because I know that you know that if you did, then you would not leave this room alive."

I breathe a sigh of relief. "Okay, so this is about me being late to take her to school. I'm honestly so sorry, I don't know what happened. I—"

"This is not about that either."

I hesitate, confused as to what else could be wrong. Maybe it's something as simple as overstepping the boundary between worker and family. After all, I'm supposed to be a live-in maid, not someone who's a member of the family at all. For some reason, this fact hurts my heart to think. Like maybe I thought I was beginning to establish a life I could be happy with. Elena's not exactly someone I imagined myself living in the same house with, but Sofia... Sofia is *exactly* what I imagined.

"No. This is about the fact that you are confusing my daughter."

I am? The confusion must show on my face, because Elena's expression hardens. She stands perfectly still, her posture rigid, like she's deciding whether to hurt me or simply walk away. There's something terrifying about her complete control.

"Sofia is in a developmental stage. She must know what is right, what is wrong, and who she can trust. That is not you."

"Whoa, hey, Elena. She can trust me. I'm—"

"Lies low from you like water from the sea," she says, scowling. "Do not think that I do not know the truth."

"The truth?"

She steps closer. I'm taller than her, but it doesn't feel like it. Her presence seems to fill the entire room, making me feel like a child all over again. I take a step back without meaning to, my spine hitting the wall.

"You think I am stupid?" Elena's voice drops to a whisper, but it's more frightening than if she'd screamed. "You think I do not see what you are doing?"

"I—"

Her eyes flash dangerously, and I go quiet. A moment of silence passes as I wait for her to make the first move. A bead of sweat forms on my brow, and begins to slowly trickle downward.

"Be glad we cannot go back in time, Morgan, to when I caught you in my house. Things would have gone very differently."

I stare at her, trying to make sense of what that means. Did she mean that she would have pulled the trigger and blown my brains out? Surely not. She must mean that she would have simply thrown me out.

"Elena, I..." my voice trails off as I see her lip curl.

"Gather your things. I want you gone. Now."

I wait for a moment, hoping that she'll take it back, say that she doesn't mean it. But her expression doesn't soften.

Instead, she continues. "I don't want to see you again. Ever. You are not welcome in my home, near my daughter, or in Cascais."

I think about what she'd said before. that if I ever hurt

Sofia, I wouldn't leave this room alive. But now I will be leaving alive, just with my heart and soul and dreams left behind in this house, along with any part left of Henry in this damned world.

Elena turns on her heel and strides from the room, leaving devastation in her wake.

What just happened?

I want to fall to my knees, to weep until there's nothing left inside me, but I know that if I did that, I'd never find the strength to stand again. And standing is all I have left.

In numb, mechanical movements, I begin to gather my few possessions. It's pathetic how little I have now: the maid's uniform Elena gave me, my pajamas, a few toiletries. Things that don't even fill my bag, along with what's left of my time at Eden. I don't take stock of any of it. I just pack everything with dead hands and an empty heart.

When I'm done, I walk out the door and head down the steps. It doesn't feel real. Not even as my footsteps echo against the walls. Not even as I rest my hand on the handle of the front door.

I pause there, my fingers wrapped around the cold metal, and look back over my shoulder. The house stretches behind me; beautiful, elegant, filled with everything I thought I wanted. What am I going to do now? Where can I possibly go?

I'm going to miss it all. The backbreaking work that somehow made me feel useful and productive. Sofia's bright laughter echoing through the halls, her small hand in mine as we walked together. Even Elena's stares, because at least they meant someone was paying attention to me, that I existed in someone's world.

And the library... I'm going to miss its floor-to-ceiling shelves and that comfortable leather chair where I'd spent my evenings. I never even finished *Mother, Mother*. I was so close to the end, dying to know how it turned out. Now I'll never know.

My throat tightens, and I force myself to turn back toward the door. This is it. Time to step back into the void and figure out how to survive on my own again.

I'm about to turn the handle when a knock vibrates against the wood from the other side.

I freeze, my hand still gripping the door. Who could be knocking here?

Nobody *ever* comes up to the house.

My heart slams in my chest. Am I supposed to call for Elena? Answer it on her behalf, like I still work here? Or answer it and walk past whoever it is?

Another knock, more insistent this time.

I glance back toward the stairs, but Elena is nowhere to be seen. With trembling fingers, I unlock the door and pull it open.

My breath leaves in a rush.

A man stands on the doorstep. Someone who should be at the bottom of the ocean, his bones picked clean by fish. But instead, his gray eyes are peering into my own.

He smiles.

Henry.

EIGHTEEN
HENRY

"Morgan."

Her name leaves my mouth like a prayer answered. Oh, it *so* feels good to have those green eyes on me again. My gaze trails from hers down to her lips. They look just like the first time I'd seen her. And just like then, all I want to do is sweep her up into my arms and kiss her. She's absolutely breathtaking.

I thought I'd have all the right words by the time I saw her. When my jet touched down in Cascais, I had them all well practiced and refined, ready to make her swoon and jump into my arms, sobbing with joy, despite whatever she's seen in the house.

But standing here now, half leaning on my cane and feeling all sorts of broken before her, I'm suddenly robbed of words. I'm speechless, taken in by the fact that standing before me is the love of my life.

She is all that matters. That truth resonates through me, pulses through every vein, reverberates through every bone in my body.

I look deep into her eyes, and I realize that what fills them isn't the joy I expected. It's something else entirely. Fear, maybe. Shock, definitely. But you know what? That's okay. It's understandable.

The last time she'd seen me, she probably thought I was going to choose Genevieve over her, that she was going to be tossed aside and killed as a stand-in wife. But that couldn't be further from the truth. I still remember how gracious and beautiful she looked, and I could never choose Genevieve over her.

No, Morgan is my one and only.

"Morgan, I..." My eyes drift downward, suddenly taking in what she's wearing. A black dress with a crisp white apron, the kind of uniform you'd see in old movies about grand houses. Like a maid. Why the hell is she dressed like a maid? My eyes go back up to hers, searching for some answer.

"Am... Am I dead?" she mutters, like she's talking to herself. She glances over her shoulder, up the stairs, like she thinks she might've died up there or something.

"No," I say, mustering up a smile despite her confusing outfit. I clear my throat, straighten my back. "Neither one of us are."

She just stares at me, her mouth slightly open, like she's trying to process something beyond comprehension. I want to reach out and touch her face, prove that I'm real, that we're both here and alive and together again.

"I know this is a shock," I say, leaning more heavily on my cane. "I know you thought I was dead. But I'm alive, Morgan. I'm alive because I had to find you."

Her eyes dart over me, taking in the cane, the scars

visible on my hands and face. I see the moment she realizes I'm really here, because her hand flies to her mouth.

"How?" she whispers.

"The fall didn't kill me, but it came close. Broken bones, internal bleeding, concussion, all of that. But I *lived*." I take a tentative step closer. "The doctors said it was a miracle. But I know what it really was. Love, Morgan. Love kept me alive."

She takes a step back, and my heart clenches.

"I've been looking for you everywhere," I continue, desperate to bridge the gap between us. "Your apartment, the library in Des Moines. I knew you'd disappear after everything that happened, but I also knew you'd go somewhere that meant something to you. And I was right, wasn't I? You came here. To Cascais."

"You... you went to Des Moines?" Something strange lingers in her voice.

"Of course. I thought you'd go back to what you knew. But when you weren't there, I realized you'd come here instead. To the place I told you about—the place I said was the most beautiful in the world."

"And you just... followed me here?"

"I followed my heart," I say, hoping to see some warmth return to her eyes. "First thing I thought of when I could think again was you. Finding you. Making sure you were safe."

Something flickers across her face. Anger, maybe? "Safe? You think I'm safe here?"

"Aren't you? You look..." I gesture at her outfit, confused. "I mean, you're working somewhere, I'm guessing? Making a bit of money while you stay in my house. That means you're safe, right?"

"Right."

There's something in her tone I don't understand, but I push forward. "Morgan, I know everything that happened was confusing. I know Eden lied to us, manipulated us. But what we felt—what we *feel*—that's real. That's the only thing that matters."

"Real?" Her voice spikes. "What part of it was real, Henry?"

"All of it. For me, all of it was real."

"The marriage," she says again, and now she's shaking. "You want to talk about marriage?"

"Yes. Our marriage. What we had, what we could still have if you'll let me—"

"Our marriage." She laughs, but there's no humor in it. "Tell me about marriage, Henry. Tell me what it means to you."

I frown, confused by the shift in her tone. "It means commitment. It means choosing someone and staying with them through everything."

"Staying with them," she repeats. "And you believe in that? You believe in faithfulness, do you?"

"Of course I do. Morgan, what's this about? I chose you. I'm here, aren't I? I came back from the *dead* for you."

"You came back from the dead," she says slowly. "How romantic. How devoted. How... faithful."

There's acid in her voice now. "Morgan, what's wrong? What happened to you here?"

My eyes drift past her, taking in the backdrop of a

house I can barely remember now. But I remember enough to know that there are photos inside that depict a truth that she should have never seen. A love that died a long time ago.

"What happened to me?" She takes a step closer, and I can see tears building in her eyes. "What happened to me is that I learned the truth. About you. About marriage. About faithfulness."

I grimace, realizing that this is very much about what she'd seen in those photos. Damn, this wasn't going at all how I'd planned.

"You're a liar, Henry. Everything you ever told me was bullshit."

"That's not true. I never lied to you about my feelings. Everything I felt for you was real."

"Your feelings," she spits. "For me. For Genevieve. How many women, Henry? How many wives?"

"Other wives?" My pulse kicks up. "Morgan, I told you. You're the only one that matters."

"Is that so?" She wipes tears from her cheeks. "I'm the only one, huh?" She shakes her head, and reaches inside her bag. Then she draws out a gun.

The world narrows to that black circle of the barrel aimed at my chest. My hands jerk upward, trembling. "Morgan, don't."

"You should have stayed dead, Henry."

A shadow shifts behind her. Before I can say anything, before I can even comprehend what's happening, I hear a sickening crack.

Morgan's eyes go wide, her pupils dilating as the gun wavers in her grip. For a split second, she looks confused, like she can't understand why the world is suddenly tilting sideways. Then her knees buckle, and she crumples onto the stone steps with a thud that turns my stomach.

The gun skitters across the ground, spinning to a stop near my feet.

Standing behind her, breathing hard and clutching a heavy iron pan, is a beautiful woman with dark hair and intense eyes. She stares down at Morgan's body. "Men Deus. She had a gun."

Then her eyes rise to meet mine, filled with complete wonder.

"Henry," she breathes. "You're alive. You're really alive."

I look back at her, the words spilling out before I can stop them.

"Who are you?"

NINETEEN
HENRY

She doesn't seem to hear me as she closes the distance between us, stepping over Morgan's unconscious form like she's nothing. I'm not sure what I expect, but it's not her throwing herself at me, her fingers tangling in my hair, her mouth finding mine with the kind of desperate hunger that suggests I should know exactly who she is.

I push her back, my hands shaking. She smiles, eyes bright with something that might be madness. Or just pure joy. I can't tell.

"You're right, now's not the time," she says, glancing down at Morgan. "We need to deal with her before Sofia sees her."

Sofia?

My throat constricts. "Who the hell is Sofia?"

She tilts her head like I've asked something amusing. "We don't have time for games, Henry."

Games? I'm not playing any games. I don't know this woman, don't know any Sofia, and they both need to be out of my house. My eyes fall to the gun at my feet, but she's already moving, snatching it up and tucking it into her belt with practiced ease.

"Take her arms," she says, bending to grip Morgan's ankles.

The command in her voice has me moving before I can think. Together, we lift Morgan. She's lighter than I expected, but my legs are already trembling without my cane. I glance back at it, abandoned by the door, but don't dare let go of Morgan to retrieve it.

"This way." She guides us toward a door beneath the stairs.

"You still haven't answered my question."

"Henry, seriously." Her voice carries an edge of impatience that scrapes against my nerves. "We don't have time for—"

A young voice drifts down from upstairs, humming some tune I don't recognize. The woman's eyes widen, panic flickering across her features.

"Hurry," she hisses.

I should drop Morgan right here. Call the police. Get this stranger and whoever's upstairs out before this gets worse. The gun is right there in her belt. I could probably wrestle it away if I had to.

But there's something in the way she speaks and looks at me. A level of familiarity that has me wondering if I've somehow forgotten something... something I should most definitely remember.

And that terrifies me more than the gun.

She leads me the rest of the way to the door, lowering Morgan's feet to the ground with careful silence. Her keys jingle softly as she fumbles through them, and I find myself wondering why this particular door needs to be locked at all.

The sound of small footsteps echoes from the stairs above.

My legs are shaking now, threatening to give out entirely as I adjust my grip on Morgan's shoulders. What the hell am I doing? This is Morgan—the woman I chose to spend the rest of my life with—and I'm helping a stranger drag her unconscious body into some hidden room.

But Morgan was going to kill me with a gun that looked eerily similar to the one that Genevieve shot me with that day on the cliff.

My chest tightens as the woman finally finds the right key. She unlocks the door and pushes it open. Darkness waits on the other side.

I feel a strange sensation, not from the darkness, but from behind me. It pulls at me, begs me to look over my shoulder, and when I do, my world tilts on its axis.

A photograph on the small table by the door. Three faces smiling back at me: myself, this dark-haired woman, and a little girl with gray eyes identical to mine.

My breath leaves in a rush. I know that face. It's my face. But I have no memory of this moment. None at all. The man in the photo looks happy, content, like he belongs with these people. Like he's home.

But I've never seen them before in my life.

"Henry." The woman's voice cuts through my shock. "Help me get her inside."

I stumble forward, my mind fracturing. Where is Genevieve in all this? This was supposed to be our vacation home, our retreat from the stresses of everyday life. But there's no trace of her anywhere. Not in the photos, not in the way this woman moves through the space like she owns it.

We maneuver Morgan through the doorway, but as I move to follow, the woman's hand slams against my chest.

"Stay out here," she says, already pulling the door closed.

"Wait, I need to make sure she's—"

The lock clicks into place.

"Open this door," I demand, rattling the handle. "That's my—"

But my words are interrupted by the sound of footsteps—lighter now, quicker—racing down the stairs behind me.

I turn, and my heart stops.

A little girl stands frozen on the bottom step, her hand gripping the bannister. She can't be more than seven or eight, with dark hair like the woman's but eyes that are unmistakably mine. Gray. Serious. And she's staring at me like she's seeing a ghost rise from the dead.

"Papai?" she whispers.

My legs buckle, and I grab the wall for support.

What... what did she just call me?

She doesn't move for a heartbeat, just stands there with tears welling in those familiar eyes. Then recognition floods her face, and she's running, flying across the space between us with a sob that sounds like pure joy mixed with desperate relief.

"Papai! Papai!"

Her small body slams into mine, knocking us both to

the floor. Sharp pain shoots up my spine from the impact, but all I can think about is this child. This... impossible child, crying into my chest with great, shuddering sobs that shake her entire frame.

I lay there, stunned, my hands hovering over her dark hair. Some instinct I don't understand makes me hold her, makes me whisper "It's okay" even though nothing about this is okay.

She pulls back to look up at me, tears streaming down her cheeks. "You came back. I knew you would. I kept your picture by my bed."

This child knows me. Loves me. Calls me Papai like it's the most natural thing in the world. But I don't remember her. I don't remember any of this.

What if I'm supposed to?

Had the fall from the cliff stolen something else from me? Like the memory of this family that seems to be so clearly mine?

"Mama!" Sofia calls suddenly, beaming with joy as she pulls me to my feet. "Mama, come quick!"

She drags me toward the stairs, but I know she's not there. I glance back toward the direction we came, and I see the woman quietly emerging from the basement door. She locks it behind her, then takes a few steps away, like she came from what looks like the kitchen.

"Henry?"

I look from the woman to the girl and back, and in that time, the most extraordinary thing happens. Her composure crumbles completely, like this is the first time she's seeing me. Her mouth parts, her eyes widen, and tears begin flowing down her cheeks.

"Henry?" Her voice breaks on my name. "Is that really you?"

"It's him, Mama!" Sofia sobs, squeezing my hand so tightly it hurts. "Papai's home! Papai came back to us!"

She presses closer to me, like I might disappear if she lets go. And God help me, holding her feels right in a way that terrifies me. Like muscle memory I can't access.

But Morgan was going to kill me with a gun that looked eerily like the one Genevieve used that day on the cliff.

Wasn't she?

The woman surges forward, and wrapping her arms around us both, the two of them begin to cry out of pure happiness. And all I can do is hug them back, while I stare at them out of confusion.

"Papai, Mama tells me you've been saving a bedtime story for me." Sofia says suddenly, looking up at me with those devastating eyes. "About the princess who lived in the tower by the sea? Can you tell it to me tonight?"

My throat tightens as I fumble for a response. But as the silence stretches, the young girl's eyes start to fall.

"You... you remember the story, do you?" she asks quietly.

"Remember what?" The words come out sharper than I intended.

The woman rests a hand on mine, and says quietly, "He remembers. He's just had a long day traveling. Isn't that right?"

When did I leave them? Why can't I remember any of this?

From behind the locked door comes a faint sound. A groan, maybe.

Her eyes snap toward the door, then back to me. There's a hint of worry in them. "Henry, you look... different since you've been gone. Are you okay?"

I'm most definitely not okay. I'm the furthest thing from okay, because I don't even know how long I've been gone, or why I left in the first place.

"Papai?" Sofia tugs at my hand, and I can hear the fear creeping into her voice. "Are you staying?"

I stare down into those gray eyes—my eyes—and realize I don't know how to answer. Because suddenly I don't know what I want anymore. I don't know who I am, or who I was, or what's real.

The sound from behind the door comes again, louder this time, but not loud enough to attract Sofia's attention.

All I know is something is very, very wrong.

And Morgan is about to wake up trapped in the dark.

TWENTY
MORGAN

The darkness presses against me. For a moment, I float in that strange space between waking and nothing, where pain exists but hasn't found me yet.

Then it hits like a sledgehammer to the back of my skull, sending waves of nausea rolling through me. I try to lift my head, but pain explodes behind my eyes, and that's when I realize I can't move my arms.

They're bound behind me, rope cutting into my wrists. I'm sitting in what feels like a wooden chair, my ankles tied to the legs.

I force my eyes open. Nothing changes. The darkness is so thick I could drown in it. I try to reach up to touch the source of the pain, but the rope around my wrists tightens when I pull. The chair creaks beneath me.

What happened?

I test the ropes, twisting my wrists, but they're too tight. Lifting my head, I fight back the nausea and try to get a look around me. But it's too dark to make out a single thing.

Where am I?

I can feel stone walls somewhere in front of me. The sound of my breathing echoes off them. But I can't reach out to explore, can't move more than a few inches in any direction. The chair feels old, wooden, with a straight back that my bound hands are pressed against.

Think, Morgan.

The memories creep back in fragments. Henry's face. Those gray eyes I'd thought were forever gone, staring at me like I was the only thing that mattered in the world.

Henry.

He's *alive*.

The realization hits me and suddenly I'm crying great, shuddering breaths that echo off stone walls. He's alive. After all this time thinking he was dead, mourning him, hating myself for clinging to the ghosts of his past, he's actually alive.

But the relief tangles with something darker. Because I remember what I was about to do. I remember the gun, cold metal against my palm, my finger hovering over the trigger.

I was going to kill him.

The thought should horrify me. Instead, it fills me with a strange satisfaction. Because he deserves it, didn't he? After all the lies, the manipulation, the way he'd used me as a stand-in wife.

He'd looked so confused when I confronted him about faithfulness. Like he couldn't understand why I was angry. Like he'd forgotten he had a wife and child living in the very house where I'd been scrubbing floors.

His maid. I'd been his *maid*.

God, how pathetic. I was so grateful for the work, so happy when Sofia called me Tia Morgan, so desperate for any scrap of family that I built a life in the ruins of his lies.

I push myself upright as much as the bonds allow, fighting the nausea. The chair scrapes against the stone floor. My fingers reach as far as possible, but there's nothing within reach.

There has to be a way out of this.

I strain my hands and arms, trying to find any give, any weakness. The chair is old, but still, it's too sturdy. And every time I move them, I hear a soft *clink*. I don't know what it is, but the more I move, the more convinced I am she's tied the ropes to something fixed.

It doesn't take me long to realize I'm not going to simply free myself. Or to realize that I must still be in the house.

The locked door. I've got to be behind there. Which means Henry is somewhere above me. Is he in on this? Laughing it up with Elena and Sofia, playing happy family? He must be, because otherwise, why am I down here? If the man I'd thought I'd married on the island had been genuine, then he would have never been okay with me being imprisoned down here.

My foot kicks something that skitters across the floor. I strain forward, but I can't reach whatever it was.

"Hello?" I call out, voice cracking. "Henry? Elena?"

The words bounce back at me. No one's coming.

"Let me out of here!"

Still nothing.

I slump back in the chair, the reality sinking in. I'd

been knocked unconscious and left here to rot. Maybe Elena or Henry will come back to check on me, to watch me waste away.

Or maybe they'll just wait until I stop being a problem.

Sofia will wonder where I went though, right? She would be smart enough to call the authorities and report me missing. Except that's wishful thinking. Sofia is a child. She'll just think I left on some extended trip.

How long does it take to die down here? Days? Weeks? Maybe this is what I get for being so desperate for love I ignored every warning sign. But even as the thought crosses my mind, I know I didn't deserve this. I didn't deserve any of it.

I deserve better than Henry Langford and his beautiful lies. I deserve better than dying alone in a basement while they play house upstairs.

The anger builds in my chest, cutting through the despair like a hot knife. I'm not going to die tied to this chair. I won't let that bastard win.

I start pulling at my bindings again, ignoring the pain, ignoring how they cut into my skin, even as my screams tear themselves from my throat.

Somehow, I'll get out of here. And when I do, I'll do what I should have done that day on the cliff.

I'll kill Henry myself.

TWENTY-ONE
HENRY

Tucking a child you don't know into bed is strange.

But not nearly as strange as reading her a bedtime story while she looks up at you like this is a dream come true. I'm not sure what I expected when I finally found Morgan. Well, that's not true. I did know. I expected us to kiss the way the *other woman* kissed me, for us to throw away everything that belonged to me and Genevieve in this house and make it ours. I expected us to finally have the happily ever after like we deserve.

Instead, it feels like I'm living that dream with someone else.

Someone named Elena, who I'm apparently madly in love with, if the pictures are anything to go by. Not to mention the child we have together. I'd always promised myself I would never have a child unless I could be wholly dedicated to her for the rest of my life. And the issue I had with Genevieve is that I never felt that way. That's why our marriage struggled, why we never had children.

I must have lost more in the fall from the cliff than I or the doctors realized. Whole years of my life, gone and forgotten.

When the story's finished and the great hero has rescued the princess in her tower, I leave Sofia's room and close the door behind me. Elena is standing with her back against the hallway wall, arms folded, thumb playing at her lips. It's not lost on me that she's devastatingly beautiful. Especially not with the way she's staring at me now.

"You don't know how long I've been waiting for this," she says, her eyes devouring me. She pushes off the wall and walks to me, running her hand over my chest and looking up into my eyes. "I wondered if you would ever come back."

I run my hand through my hair as discomfort rolls through me. I give her a nervous smile and take a step back, putting distance between us.

"Look," I say, putting my hands up, wincing as I lean wrong on my injured leg. It really is too early for me to be off the cane. "You should know something."

She closes the distance between us again. This time, she presses her body against mine, leans in, and whispers, "Come to bed."

My body reacts before my mind can stop it.

Oh, God.

"I don't remember you," I blurt out, my cheeks burning with shame. I am a man, after all, and these things can't always be controlled. But the woman I love is locked away downstairs. Maybe I agreed to the Stand-In Wife thing. Maybe I've got a second wife hidden in some vacation house. But that's beside the point. I'm not going to cheat on Morgan.

Elena freezes.

Panic shoots through my veins. I worry for a moment about what my supposed wife—is that what she is?—will think. Then the corner of her mouth lifts into a smile and she takes a step back, relaxing.

"I know," she says simply.

I blink. "You know?"

"Of course I know, Henry," she says. "I'm not a fool. I can tell the difference when you look at me now compared to how you used to look at me."

For some reason, the way she says that makes me a little sad. There's something in her voice, like she's been watching me this whole time, seeing that I don't know her.

"I... We used to know each other well?"

She snorts, shaking her head as she walks down the hallway. I follow, listening as she speaks without turning around. "Knew each other well? Henry, we were madly in love. You used to spend every second of the day with me." She pauses at a doorway, glancing back over her shoulder with a sly smile. "You were obsessed."

"I was?"

The word comes out smaller than I want it to. Hard to imagine being obsessed with anyone when I can't even remember my own life.

She pushes open the bedroom door and steps inside. I hesitate at the doorway, suddenly aware that I'm about to enter what was apparently our most private space. She notices and rolls her eyes. "This is *our* room, Henry."

I step inside and look around. The space feels lived-in but completely foreign. A king-sized bed dominates the room, dark wood frame with intricate carvings. The sheets are immaculately made. At the sides, there are matching nightstands, with a large dresser against the far wall.

But it's the photos that stop me. They're everywhere. On the dresser, the nightstands, even hanging on the walls. Picture after picture of us together. Elena and me at dinner, laughing. The two of us on a beach somewhere, her in a white dress, my arm around her waist. Sofia as a baby, sleeping between us in this very bed.

A whole life. And I remember none of it.

A woman's robe hangs on the back of the door. When I glance toward the closet, I can see it's split down the middle. Women's clothes on one side, men's on the other. Shirts I apparently own, shoes that must be my size.

This was a home I could have easily seen myself and Morgan living in. Hell, it could have been perfect for myself and Eve too. But instead... it's all *her*. Elena.

"I... Look, there's something I should tell you," I say.

"Is this about Morgan?" Her tone shifts instantly. Sharp. Hostile. I get the feeling I shouldn't say too much. Any married woman would react badly to hearing about another woman. Her eyes narrow. "I know something happened between you two while you were away. She denies it, but I *know*."

There's something dangerous in her voice now, and it makes the hair on my neck stand up.

"What did she tell you?"

"Only that the two of you were... friends." She spits

the word like it tastes bad. "But I'm not stupid, Henry. I see the way she looks when your name comes up."

"She said that?" The disappointment hits harder than it should. Friends. After everything we went through, that's how she described us. But then I realize... of course she would say that. She was working for a woman I was supposed to have a family with. She was trying to survive.

Elena crosses her arms, studying my face. "All I care about is what *you* think and feel. So... were you just friends?"

I nod slowly. The lie sits heavy on my tongue. "Yes. We were just friends." The words taste like ash. "I'm... struggling to remember everything though. While I was away, I was injured. I fell off a cliff and... yeah, it wasn't good."

Elena's expression softens immediately. The hostility melts away. She comes to me with careful steps, like she's approaching something wounded. When she reaches me, she presses a gentle kiss to my cheek. Her lips are warm, soft.

"I'm sorry," she whispers. "I shouldn't have been so harsh. I was just... I've been so scared, Henry. When you didn't come home, when *years* passed with no word, I thought I'd lost you forever."

Years?

Her voice breaks slightly. "And then when you did come back, you didn't know us. It felt like losing you all over again."

I want to comfort her, but I don't know how. Don't know what words would mean something to her.

"I'll tell you everything tomorrow," she continues.

"About us, about what happened before you left, about the life we built together. But it's late now." She glances toward the bed. "Come to bed, Henry. Please for me, por favor."

She moves to the dresser, pulling out silk pajamas. There's something graceful about the way she moves through this space, like she's done this hundreds of times before. I try to look away as she changes, studying the photos on the nightstand instead, but there's something magnetic about her. The way she exists in this space that's supposed to be ours. I find myself stealing glances, noticing the curve of her shoulder as she slips out of her dress, the way her hair falls across her back.

When she's done, she slips into bed and gives me a look like this is an age old routine. The mattress dips under her weight, and she pats the space beside her.

I hesitate.

"Don't worry about your clothing. I will wash the sheets tomorrow. Just come to bed."

I listen and obey, lying down next to her. The sheets smell like lavender and something else. Rose layered with an undercurrent of musk. My breath catches in my chest, because *that* smell, I know. It smells like the perfume I'd given Morgan, and Eve before her.

I must be the biggest douchebag on earth.

She doesn't try to touch me beyond what's necessary, just curls into my arm like it's natural. Her body fits against mine perfectly. But it doesn't feel right.

I lie there listening to her breathe, feeling the warmth of her body against mine. She's beautiful, that's undeniable. And clearly, we had something real once. But all I can think about is Morgan, locked away somewhere beneath us in the dark.

Elena shifts slightly, her breathing starting to even out. "Herry?" she murmurs.

"Yeah?"

"I love you. I never stopped loving you, even when you were gone."

The words hang in the air. I know she's waiting for me to say it back, but I can't. Not when I don't remember what that love felt like. Not when my heart belongs to someone else.

"Get some sleep," I whisper instead.

She makes a soft sound that might be disappointment, but within minutes her breathing settles into sleep. I wait, counting her breaths, making sure she's truly out before I dare to move.

When I'm certain she won't wake, I carefully extract myself from her arms. She murmurs something in Portuguese but doesn't wake. I wait another few minutes, then begin searching the room quietly.

Her keys have to be here somewhere. I can't leave Morgan in the basement. It doesn't matter that I'd gotten caught up in the moment by all the confusion of me having a child and another wife. It was a mistake to even allow it to happen.

I start with the dresser, moving carefully through jewelry and personal items. Nothing. The nightstand is next. I'm sliding open the drawer, feeling around books and what feels like a small bottle of pills.

And then there they are. The small ring of keys I'd seen her use before.

I slip them into my pocket and quietly make my way to the door. The hallway is dark now, just faint moonlight filtering through the windows. But I know where I'm going.

The locked door under the stairs.

My hands shake as I try different keys. Every sound feels impossibly loud in the quiet house. The first key doesn't fit. Neither does the second. My heart pounds as I try the third, then the fourth.

Finally, one turns. The door opens with a soft click.

Nothing but darkness ahead. I feel along the wall for a light switch but find nothing except cold stone. My fingers trace the rough texture as I step forward, finding what feels like stone steps leading down.

I take them one at a time, leaning heavily on the wall for support. My injured leg protests with each step, but I push through the pain. The air grows colder as I descend, and I start to smell something sickly sweet.

That's when my head connects with something hard. A low wooden beam I couldn't see in the dark.

I curse beneath my breath, stumbling forward and catching myself against the stone wall.

And from somewhere in the darkness below, I hear it.

Morgan's voice.

"Henry?"

"Morgan," I whisper into the blackness, taking another careful step down. My injured leg throbs, but I push through the pain. "Are you okay?"

Silence stretches between us. Then her voice cuts through the darkness.

"Oh, you care now?" Her words drip with venom. "How touching."

Relief floods through me at hearing her voice, followed immediately by the sharp sting of her tone. I feel along the wall, searching for anything that might help me see in this blackness.

"Of course I care. I came to—"

"To what?" she interrupts.

"Morgan..."

A bitter laugh echoes from somewhere in the darkness. "Oh, don't play dumb, Henry. Not now. I know what I am to you."

I find what feels like another step and take it, my hand still searching the stone wall. The air down here is thick and stale, carrying that sickly sweet smell I'd noticed before.

"You're my wife," I say quietly.

"I'm your Stand-In Wife," she spits back. "There's a difference. Though I suppose you'd know all about that, wouldn't you? Since you signed that contract."

My blood turns to ice. I wish I could say I didn't know what contract she was talking about, but the sad truth is that I do. At the time, though, when I signed it, a Stand-In Wife was just a concept. Not a real person. Not someone I loved.

"You lying, cheating bastard," Morgan continues, her voice breaking. "I wish you'd never come back from that fall. I wish you were dead."

The words tear through me, but I deserve every one of them. I take another step down, desperate to reach her, to somehow make this right.

"Morgan, please—"

"Don't." Her voice is deadly quiet now. "Don't you dare. You don't get to 'please' me anymore. You used me. You made me fall in love with you while planning to throw me away the whole time."

"That's not... I didn't mean to—"

"Don't lie to me! You made me feel like I was special, like I was chosen. When all along, you were hiding not *one* wife, but *two*."

I try to picture where she is in this darkness, moving slowly toward the sound of her voice. The basement feels small but cold, the stone walls seeming to press in around us.

"Don't come any closer," she warns.

But I take one careful step forward, then another, until I think I'm close enough to reach out. My fingers brush against what feels like her shoulder, and she jerks away.

I breathe a sigh of relief. It's one thing to hear her voice. It's another to touch her.

"I'm going to get you out of here," I tell her.

"I don't want your help. I don't want *anything* from you."

I pull my hands back, settling back on my heels in the dark. Even without being able to see her face, I can feel the hatred radiating from her. "I can't just leave you here."

"Why not? You think I'll tell everyone about Eden? About how you planned to throw away my life like it meant nothing?"

The blood drains from my face. Something like that would not only have a significant impact on the businesses in my portfolio, but would put us both seriously at risk. And after coming so close to dying, I know I'm not ready to go yet.

She scoffs at my silence.

Something about it sets me on edge, and for the first time, I raise my voice. "Will you stop being so difficult?"

She goes quiet.

"I care about you, damn it."

A beat passes, then her voice comes in a soft tone. "You lied to me."

"I'm prepared to spend the rest of my life making it up to you."

"I'll never forgive you," she says, but her voice wavers.

"Then I'll spend every day happily trying, even if it's in vain."

Another beat passes. Then she whispers, "Just get me out of here."

I breathe a sigh of relief and rush forward, my hands feeling in and around the tied ropes. At first, I think it's going to be an easy job. But then I feel how expertly they're tied. And then I feel the cold touch of a metal lock.

My face falls as I realize that this isn't just tied rope. Somehow, Elena's got it all running through a lock; a lock that she has the key to.

For a moment, my heart lifts as I scramble for the keys in my pocket. I fumble through them, fitting each one to the lock, but slowly, the hope I felt begins to die as each key fails.

"What's taking so long?" she asks.

I growl to myself, "She's got a lock fitted to it and I don't have the key."

Morgan curses, and I can only agree wholeheartedly with the sentiment. This isn't ideal. But it's not a big deal. I'll simply go upstairs, wake Elena, and demand that she give me the right key.

We're not savages. We're not going to keep a woman imprisoned in the basement. Even if I'm sure that Elena had good intentions, after seeing how Morgan was about to murder me.

"I'll be back," I say, stuffing the keys back into my pocket. "I'm going to get you out of here."

"Why?" The question comes out broken, vulnerable. "Why are you doing this when a whole *family* is waiting for you?"

I wish I could see her face, wish I could show her how much I mean what I'm about to say. "Because somewhere between the lies and the manipulation and the therapeutic bullshit," I say, my voice rough with emotion, "I fell in love with you. Really in love. Not because you reminded me of someone else or because you were convenient or because you were part of the program. But because you're *you*, Morgan. Because you're real."

For a moment, there's only silence in the darkness. Then I hear her breath catch, and I know my words have reached her, even if she won't admit it.

"Go screw yourself," she whispers, but I can hear the tears in her voice.

I get to my feet, my leg screaming in protest. "I love you," I say, finally speaking the words I've whispered every time I stared in the mirror, practicing what I would say to her. "I'm in love with you."

"I hate you," she responds, but her voice wavers.

I turn to go. But as I reach the stairs, I hear something else. Her voice, so quiet I almost miss it:

"God I hate that I love you too."

The words hit me square in the chest, filling me with equal parts hope and despair. Because now I know that some part of her still loves me, and that upstairs, another woman and child love me too.

That makes what I have to do next infinitely harder.

TWENTY-TWO
HENRY

The basement door clicks shut behind me. I lean my head against it, trying to settle into the thought that I had been that man. The one who had a family. The one who finally came home to them only to reveal that he was leaving them for another woman.

But I have no choice. It's not my fault that I forgot them. It's not my fault that I fell in love with her. Morgan is everything, and life is too short to do myself a disservice by spending it with a wife and child that I don't even know.

That might make me an awful person. But that's something I'll have to live with, because at least I'll be happy.

With my hand trailing along the wall for support, I walk through the hall to the base of the stairs. I stare up the long ascent into darkness, where I know that I'll wake a woman and destroy every hope she's carried in her heart for the last… I don't even know how long it's been since I left them. Either way, what I'm about to do will absolutely kill her.

Her and Sofia.

My little girl.

I draw another shaking breath, and suddenly decide that now's the perfect time for a cigarette. I limp toward the front door, quietly step outside, and lower myself onto the first step. Reaching inside my pocket, I withdraw a cigarette and light it.

Within moments, I feel the sweet relief of nicotine flooding my system. I close my eyes and revel in the taste of my Camel smokes, and the smell of smoke wafting through the air. I breathe out, watching a cloud of it drift upward toward the stars, out toward the vast expanse of ocean in the far distance, all of it visible by moonlight.

I'm not sure how long I sit there, staring out over the distance. The only measure of time I have are the small butts of cigarettes sitting on the ground beneath me. My eyes drift forward, looking over the yard, until I see my cane lying in the grass. I grunt happily and stumble forward, pick up my cane, and finish off my last cigarette, deciding that it's time.

With a heavy heart, I turn back toward the front door. It opens easily, the dark foyer swallowing me. I step inside.

The front door shuts behind me.

I start toward the stairs, the slow tap of my cane nothing like the beating drum of my heart.

"Papai?"

I freeze at the bottom of the stairs and glance to the side. Sofia's standing in the doorway off the foyer, her hands clasped together and her eyes big and wide, like she's still in disbelief that I'm here. My hand tightens on the cane, unsure what to say.

It doesn't seem right that I break her heart first, before I've broken her mother's.

"Hey... kid," I say, wincing even as the words spill from my mouth. Kid? I'm already playing the part of an unloving father, when that's not even the truth. I'm sure I could love her. But I just don't know her. I point awkwardly up the stairs. "Shouldn't you be in bed?"

"I couldn't sleep." She steps forward, out of the darkness and into the moonlight spilling in from the windows over the front door. "Where did you go?"

Ah, I see tears in her eyes now. She thought that I left. My heart cracks a little, knowing that this is what she'll look like when I eventually do. I glance away, knowing that if I stare into those eyes any longer, my resolve might break.

"I just went out for a smoke."

"Smoking is bad for you."

The bluntness of her words catches me by surprise, and I can't help but chuckle at them. "That's right. Don't ever make the mistake of picking up a cigarette. They'll kill you."

Her eyes widen as she steps even closer. "Really?"

I nod. "Most definitely."

Her hands wring together, just as nervous as I am. Somehow, that makes me feel a little more comfortable. I turn and sit at the bottom of the stairs, patting the space next to me. She sits next to me, her little knees pressed together as she folds her hands in her lap, giving the impression that she's far more mature than her years suggest.

"Do you think Mama smokes?"

"I don't know. But I don't think so."

She hums to herself, like she thought the same. Then she turns and looks up at me, like she's studying me. She reaches out and brushes her hand against the cane. "Where did you go?"

"I told you. Just out for a smoke."

Her face scrunches up, and her brows furrow. "That's not what I meant."

Then I realize. She's asking me, where did I *go*.

"Oh." It hits me then, how children can see straight through you without even trying. She's not asking about my leaving to smoke outside. She's asking about the years I was gone. I clear my throat. "Well, you see, I uh... I had business that took me away."

Her face turns away from me, and she begins to pick at a loose thread from her pajamas. "You were gone muito tempo."

I'm not sure what that means. But I must have once, right? I must have known some Portuguese. I close my eyes. Whatever memories I lost from the fall don't matter. They don't change the fact that I left her and Elena for someone else. They don't change the fact that I'm a horrible father, whether I remember being one or not. The amnesia doesn't make me innocent.

"Yeah, I... I'm sorry."

"But you're back now."

"I am." I wince too late, realizing what I said. *Am* I

back? In a physical manner of speaking, yeah, I am, but I'm not really, am I?

She looks up at me then, and the words that come out of her mouth stop my heart cold. "You shouldn't be."

I stare at her, my mouth opening and closing like a fish. Finally, I manage to get words out. "What do you mean by that?"

She doesn't answer me.

"Sofia?" The name feels foreign on my tongue, but also somehow... right. I try not to think about that, instead leaning toward her and bumping her gently with my shoulder. I try to make it playful. I'm not sure it works. "Should I go ask your mother about that?"

That gets her attention. Her gaze snaps to mine, wide and panicked. She shakes her head frantically. "No, don't do that."

"Why not?" I smile now, despite myself. And I begin to wonder then if maybe I'm making a mistake. Not in choosing Morgan over everything else—that could never be a mistake—but in the idea of just abandoning Sofia too. Maybe I could work out some sort of shared custody arrangement with Elena. After all, Sofia's supposed to be my daughter, right? Shouldn't I at least *try* to be a good father?

"Don't wake Mama at night. She gets angry."

I laugh then, despite myself. My voice echoes across the foyer and she quickly puts her hand over my mouth. Somehow, that only makes it funnier, but I get the message. Stay quiet. Don't wake Mama. I nod, but she doesn't let go of my mouth until I reach up and gently pull her hand away. I give her a smile.

"I get it," I say quietly. "Don't want to wake Mama bear."

"*Never* wake Mama." She says this with such intensity that it stops me cold. She leans in closer. "Promise."

My smile falters. There's something in her voice.

"I mean it!"

"Okay. I promise."

She audibly breathes a sigh of relief, her shoulders slumping as the tension leaves her body. She eyes me with a sideways glance, like she's trying to decide if she can trust me.

"What is it?"

She bites her lip. It's a sort of funny and unnatural expression on her face, like it's something she picked up off TV, but it's endearing. Then, in a rush of words, she asks, "Would you read to me?"

"Read to you?"

She nods quickly, "Just one time."

My smile returns. It's not a great idea, considering how I'm about to go and break her mother's heart that I'm not staying, which will inevitably break Sofia's heart too. But there's something about the way she asks—hopeful but prepared for rejection—that gets to me. Maybe this is where I can start being a real father. "Okay, take me to your book."

She grabs me by the hand and pulls me off the steps and after her. I stumble with my cane as I try to keep up, suddenly regretting my choice as my body twinges in uncomfortable pain. It's not long before she leads me to a small library and pushes me into a reading chair.

A thread of memory pulls at me, and it's strange. I

remember this room. I remember these books lining the shelves, the way the lamplight hits the spines just so. Before I can process the thought any further, Sofia's gone and fetched a fairy tale off the bottom shelf. She races back, jumping into my lap without warning.

I bite my tongue hard, my eyes watering with pain. I count in my head—one, two, three—waiting for the sharp ache in my leg to subside as Sofia flips through the pages, seemingly reaching a point where she'd stopped before. When she looks up at me, there's something I can only describe as complete love in her eyes; the kind of pure, uncomplicated adoration that only children can give. It hits me square in the chest, unexpected and overwhelming. For a moment, I can almost understand what I lost when I forgot her. What I may lose again when I speak to Elena.

"Here," she points to the page with a small finger. "Read here."

I let go of a heavy breath, pushing the count in my head and the pain aside. I take the little book from her and really look at her face, seeing the way her eyes light up with anticipation. "You don't want me to start at the beginning?"

She shakes her head, her dark hair whipping back and forth across my shoulder. "No. This is where Morgan left off."

"Morgan?" The name catches me off guard. "She read to you too?"

She nods solemnly. "She didn't finish the story. I think she's gone. Mama got mad."

I don't say anything. What can I say? That Morgan's

not gone, just locked in the basement? That she's waiting for me to come back and save her?

"Why did she get in trouble?"

She just scrunches up her face, like she's trying to find words for something too big to explain. She doesn't answer me, just points back to the story with that serious expression children get when something really matters to them.

So I begin to read.

The words come easier than I expected. It's a story about a lost prince who can't remember his kingdom, and the irony isn't lost on me. Sofia settles against me as I read, warm and trusting, her breathing gradually slowing. I find myself getting lost in the rhythm of the sound of my own voice, the weight of her small body against mine, the way she occasionally points to a picture or makes a small sound of delight.

This must be what I forgot. This quiet intimacy. This simple love. When I finally close the book, she's drowsy but still awake, blinking up at me with heavy eyes.

"Did you like the ending?" I ask.

She nods sleepily. "The prince remembered."

Yeah. The prince remembered.

I lift her carefully, surprised by how light she is, holding her to me with one arm while gripping my cane with the other. I leave the book on the side table and carry her toward the stairs. Each step is a small agony, my leg screaming in protest, my back aching from the awkward angle. But I manage.

Her room is at the top of the stairs, decorated in soft pastels with stuffed animals scattered everywhere. I place her gently in bed and pull the covers up to her chin. She's already half-asleep, but she reaches out and catches my hand before I can leave.

"Papai?"

"Yeah?"

"Will you be here tomorrow?"

The question is a knife to the chest. Because the answer is no. Tomorrow I'll tell Elena I'm leaving with Morgan. It doesn't mean that I won't see Sofia again, but... who knows how things will go? I know that a battle with a judge likely wouldn't go well. Even with all the money I have to throw at a court case, I know that no judge or jury could completely ignore how I'd seemingly abandoned Elena and Sofia for years on end.

"Get some sleep," I whisper instead.

She nods and closes her eyes, her grip on my hand loosening. I wait until her breathing deepens before I carefully extract myself and head back down the hall.

When I push open what I assume is my bedroom door, I see Elena lying there, asleep. Her dark hair spreads across the pillow like spilled ink, and she looks peaceful. Beautiful, even.

But all I can think about is Morgan. She's still down there in that basement, tied up, no doubt wondering if I meant what I said about loving her. Wondering if I'm coming back or if I've already chosen my forgotten family over her. Maybe even wondering if she'll have a chance to try and kill me again.

Thoughts like that can destroy a person's love. And wanting anything but that, I start forward, reaching to wake Elena.

But then Sofia's warning rings in my head, sounding like an alarm bell. *Don't wake her. Never wake Mama.*

I shake my head and back away from the bed. Whatever conversation I need to have with Elena can wait until morning. It has to wait. Morgan's just going to have to hold on a little longer.

The thought makes me feel like shit, but what choice do I have?

I eye the armchair in the corner, all leather, overstuffed, and probably expensive as hell. It'll have to do. I'm not sleeping next to Elena. Not when Morgan's so close.

I settle into the chair with a grunt, propping my cane against the armrest. The leather creaks under my weight. I close my eyes, telling myself I'll just rest them for a moment. Just until morning comes and I can figure out how to untangle this mess I've found myself in.

But exhaustion hits me like a freight train, and I'm asleep within minutes, dreaming of fairy tale princes who remember their kingdoms and little girls who ask if you'll be there tomorrow.

TWENTY-THREE
MORGAN

I wait.
    And I wait.
    But he doesn't come.

TWENTY-FOUR
HENRY

The dream starts the way they all do now. With her.

Morgan straddles my hips, her weight settling against me like she belongs there. Her hair falls around us, blocking out everything else, so that it's me and her in this eternal moment.

"I've been waiting," she whispers.

Her hands trace down my chest, over my stomach. And though we're both still clothed, even though I still feel that lingering ache from my injuries, every nerve ending comes alive. The bruises, the broken ribs, the leg that still throbs... none of it matters when she touches me like this. I want her. *Need* her in a way that makes my chest tight with desperation.

My hands find her waist, pulling her closer. My breath shudders as she leans downs and kisses that spot just below my ear that makes me lose all rational thought. Her body moves in perfect rhythm that reminds me of the very first night we slept together: our wedding night.

This is right. This is how it should be. Not complicated. Not twisted up in lies and forgotten memories. Just *us*.

"Henry," she whispers against my ear. "I love you."

The words send electricity through me. I pull her closer, desperate to feel more, to have *more*.

But something's off. The voice doesn't sound quite right. It's too...

"Henry."

The voice is softer now, different. *Wrong.*

My eyes snap open.

Elena hovers above me, half-undressed, her dark hair falling over bare shoulders. Her hands are on my chest, her body pressed against mine in a way that makes my stomach lurch with confusion and guilt. The dream shatters around me like broken glass.

"What the hell?" I push her off me, more roughly than I intend. She stumbles backward, catching herself against the bed.

"Henry, what—" Her face scrunches up in confusion, hurt flashing in her eyes. "I thought you were awake. You were saying my name."

Was I? The thought makes me sick.

"I'm sorry, I just—" I fumble over the words, my brain still trying to separate dream from reality. My body is still responding to what I thought was Morgan's touch, and the shame of it burns through me. "You startled me. My injuries, they're still..." I gesture vaguely at my leg, my ribs, anywhere that might explain why I just shoved her away from me.

Her expression immediately softens, the hurt replaced by sympathy. She fixes her clothing and moves toward me carefully, like I'm a wounded animal that might bolt, and presses a gentle kiss to my cheek. The gesture is tender, loving, and it makes the guilt worse.

"I'm sorry," she murmurs. "I should have been more careful. I just missed you so much."

The tenderness in her voice makes my chest tight. She smoothes down her hair with practiced movements.

"I made food," she says, her tone deliberately light. "Your favorite."

My favorite? I have no idea what that might be, but I suppose she would know.

It hits me then that Morgan is still tied up in that basement, waiting for me to come back. Waiting for me to prove that I chose her.

With a grimace, I fix my shirt and adjust myself, before following Elena downstairs, my cane tapping against each step. The sound echoes through the quiet house, marking time like a countdown. Each tap reminds me of my weakness, my dependence. My eyes drift to the basement door as we pass.

How long has it been? The sunlight streaming through the windows is bright and harsh, suggesting it's nearly midday. Morgan's been down there all night, tied up in the dark, thinking I broke my promise.

Elena leads me to the kitchen, where the smell of... something *delicious* fills the air. It's familiar, and I know I've had it before. But what is it?

Elena sets a plate at the bar, smiles, and says, "Bacalhau à brás. Just the way you like it, sim?"

I take a seat and look skeptically at the dish. I'm hesitant, but when I take a bite, the flavours explode across my tongue. It's incredible, absolutely incredible. I remember having it, but I don't remember... No. I've sat at this bar before. The image is fuzzy, but warm. I can remember Elena's voice now, just distantly. And there's life in the home.

The guilt hits harder now. Not just for Morgan, but for what I'm about to do to Elena. To Sofia. They seem so happy with me, and God knows it's been a long time since I've felt that kind of familial happiness from *anyone*. My last few years with Eve weren't exactly great.

"You didn't sleep in bed last night," Elena says, settling next to me with her own plate. "You were hurting, não?"

I take another bite, buying time. The food tastes like ash now, despite how perfectly it's prepared. "A little, yeah."

"What happened to you out there, Henry? When you left, I mean." She leans forward slightly, concern creasing her brow.

The question hangs between us. I could tell her everything. About Eve, about our attempt to save our marriage, and how it ended up with me falling in love with another woman and getting shot off the cliffside. But looking at her face—this beautiful woman who clearly loves me, who's been waiting for me to come home—I can't bring myself to destroy her world with the truth.

"It's complicated," I say instead.

"Complicated how?" There's an edge to her voice now, something that suggests she won't be put off easily. "Henry, after Sofia was born, you disappeared for years. I didn't know if you were alive or dead. Now you're back, and you won't even tell me what happened? Por favor, I need to understand."

After Sofia was born?

I lower my fork to the plate, press my fingers to my temples in an attempt to stop the headache from coming on. But I fail. The migraine sets in deep as I struggle to remember. My struggles with Eve lasted long enough that I suppose it would have been possible for me to find time here with Elena; time enough to have a child.

But still... years? How did Elena manage? She must have *lived* on the hope that I would come back to her.

"Look, Elena," I set down my fork, the food suddenly impossible to swallow. "There's something I need to tell you."

She goes still, fork halfway to her mouth. Something in my tone must alert her that this isn't going to be good news. "What is it?"

"I want to let Morgan go."

The words hang in the air between us. Elena's face goes blank, processing what I just said.

"Let her go?" She sets the utensil down with deliberate care, like she's trying to control herself. "Henry, that woman tried to kill you. With a gun."

"There was some confusion. A misunderstanding."

"A misunderstanding?" Her voice rises slightly, and I can see the effort it takes for her to keep it controlled.

"Yes, a *misunderstanding*. It's not right, keeping her locked up like that." I lean forward, trying to make her understand. "We have to let her go. We're not savages."

"You're right, we will let her go. When the police arrive."

My mouth works as I try to find a response. "When the police arrive? You called the police?"

"Yes, Henry. I did."

I shake my head, "No, no. I don't want her to get in trouble."

Something dangerous flickers in Elena's eyes. The soft, sympathetic woman from moments ago is disappearing, replaced by something harder. Colder.

"Why?" she asks quietly, but there's steel in her voice now. "Why does she mean so much to you?"

"She doesn't—"

"Não me minta." Her voice cuts through my protest like a knife. "You were supposed to be friends, right? That's what you told me when I asked about her. So why are you so desperate to save her?"

I can feel the situation spiraling, can see the trap closing around me, but I don't know how to stop it. The Elena sitting across from me now isn't the gentle, loving wife who made me bacalhau à brás. This is someone else entirely. Someone who's managed to raise Sofia on her own for years without a husband to help.

"Look, please—"

"Please what?" She leans back in her chair, studying me with those dark eyes. "What is it about this woman that makes you willing to risk nossa família?"

My tongue darts across my lips nervously. This conversation wasn't going at all like I'd planned. "I…"

"Papai? Mama?"

We both freeze. Sofia stands in the doorway, rubbing her eyes with one small fist. Her pajamas are wrinkled, her dark hair sticking up at odd angles. She looks between Elena and me, those gray eyes—my eyes—picking up on the tension even in her sleepy state.

Elena's transformation is instant. The dangerous edge disappears from her voice, replaced by motherly warmth. It's so smooth, so practiced, that it sends a chill down my spine.

"Bom dia, querida," she says in a gentle tone. "Did you sleep well?"

Sofia nods, but her gaze lingers on me. Something passes through her eyes, before she walks over to Elena. She's holding something in her free hand.

"Mama?" she asks quietly. "I found this in Morgan's room."

Elena takes whatever Sofia is holding, her face going pale as she examines it. When she looks up at me, her eyes are full of an emotion I can't quite read. Betrayal. Rage?

"Why don't you go back to your room and get dressed for the day, Sofia?"

Sofia hesitates, her eyes passing from her mother to me, but slowly, she nods. She turns and goes without a word.

When the sound of her footsteps has faded, Elena faces me, holding something for me to see.

"What is this, Henry?"

There, catching the morning light streaming through the window, is a ring.

Morgan's wedding ring.

TWENTY-FIVE
MORGAN

I can't see anything.

Down here in the dark, it's impossible to know how much time has passed. The darkness swallows everything. Time, hope, the sound of my own voice when I scream Henry's name until my voice gives out completely. Now when I try to yell, nothing comes out but this horrible rasping sound. Like an animal dying.

He's not coming.

My head hangs in exhaustion. All I want is sleep, but my body's in too uncomfortable a position to allow it. And even if I was comfortable, my throat's squeezing painfully out of thirst. I don't remember the last time I drank anything, or even ate anything. With my tongue feeling like sandpaper, I suddenly feel like I know what it means to die of thirst.

I would kill to have a last meal at Café do Horizonte. One of Catarina's fresh orange juices... I tug weakly at the rope, but there's no give. Briefly, I wonder if Elena or Henry will ever come back down here and at least put me out of my misery. Or will they choose to ignore me, pretend I don't exist, and let me die the hard way?

Catarina had warned me. What was it she had said?

That house should be burned to the ground. It brings nothing but death and sorrow to anyone who enters.

My brow furrows as her words fill my mind, as fresh as the day I heard them.

That house... it devours people.

If only I had known just how true those words would be. My train of thought is disturbed by the sound of footsteps above me.

My heart stops, then starts hammering so hard I can feel it in my throat. Multiple people walking around up there. Voices I can't make out, but the tone is wrong. Angry. Urgent.

The footsteps get louder. Coming toward the basement door, until it finally opens. The darkness lightens a shade, just enough for me to make out an outline of my surroundings: a small room with nothing in it except for what looks like a few boxes stacked in the corner.

"Move. Agora."

The sound of Elena's voice draws my attention back to the stairs. It's cold as winter.

"Elena, please—"

Henry's voice. Desperate.

"I said move. Vai!"

Heavy footsteps on the stairs. Someone limping, stumbling. When I force my eyes open, squinting against the light, I can see shapes. Elena's behind someone, pushing them down the stairs.

Henry.

He looks like hell. His face is gray, covered in sweat, and he's favoring his bad leg so badly he can barely walk, even with a cane. Behind him, Elena has something in her hand that makes my blood turn to ice.

A gun.

More specifically, *my* gun. She's pointing it at his back like he's a criminal. Like he's nothing.

"All the way down," she says, her voice deadly calm. "Go stand next to your other wife."

Other wife.

I have a feeling I won't be leaving this basement alive.

Henry stumbles down the last few steps and catches himself against the stone wall. His breathing is ragged, like every step hurts. Elena kicks him hard in the back without warning, and he goes down like a sack of rocks. His bad leg crumples and he hits the ground with a sound that makes me flinch.

"Elena, stop—" I croak out, but she swings the gun toward me so fast I think she might shoot me right now.

"Cala a boca," she snarls. "You don't get to talk. You don't get to breathe unless I say so."

Henry's trying to get up, his face twisted in pain. There's a dark bruise spreading across his left cheek, and his lip is split and bleeding. She must have beaten him with that gun upstairs.

"Get up," Elena commands. "Get up and go stand next to her."

Henry pushes himself up slowly, like an old man. Despite how dark it is, when he gets close to me, I can see everything in his eyes. The guilt that's eating him alive.

The fear that he's going to watch me die. But something else too. Something that looks like... love.

Maybe he didn't choose them over me after all.

"Seven years," she says, and her voice is shaking with pure rage. "Seven years I waited for you, Henry. Seven years I raised our daughter alone, telling her bedtime stories about her Papai who would come home someday."

The gun moves between Henry and me, and I realize I'm holding my breath.

"And you were off, sleeping with the likes of *her?*" She spits the words like poison.

"Elena, please—" Henry starts.

"Cala-te!" She pistol whips him, silencing him with a heavy grunt.

She turns the gun back to me, and I'm staring down the barrel. It's bigger than I thought it would be.

"You want to know what really angers me?" Elena's voice is conversational now, which somehow makes it a thousand times worse. "It's not even that you left us. Men leave all the time. I could have handled that. But you replaced me."

"I didn't know—" Henry says desperately.

"You didn't know?" Elena throws back her head and laughs, but it's the kind of laugh that makes your skin crawl. "You didn't know you had a family waiting for you? You didn't know you had a daughter who cried herself to sleep some nights wondering if her Papai was ever coming home?"

"The accident—"

"Oh, the accident!" Elena's voice drips with venom. "You truly are pathetic, Henry. I should have seen it right from the start. But do not worry. A little time down here might set you right. Remind you to appreciate what matters."

I can see Henry's jaw working as he struggles for words that might save us. The gun hasn't moved from my face.

"I know how you feel," I breathe out slowly, trying to steady myself as my gaze lifts from the barrel to meet Elena's eyes. I wince, as I dry swallow, trying to get my voice to work. But I don't have a choice. I force the words out. "I thought I was the only one married to Henry. But I wasn't. There was Genevieve."

The reaction is immediate and terrifying. She jabs the barrel into my forehead, hard enough to draw a gasp of pain from me, and she holds it there.

"There is no Eve. There's only me. I am Henry's wife!" she screams, spit flying from her lips.

The pure hatred in her voice makes my bladder want to let go. But all I can think is the fact that she called her *Eve*. She knows her.

She presses the gun against my temple, hard enough to hurt. The metal is so cold it burns. This is it. This is really it. I'm going to die in this basement, tied to a chair, and no one will ever know what happened to me.

"Elena, please," Henry's voice breaks completely. "If you're going to kill someone, kill me. She didn't know about you. She didn't know about Sofia. This isn't her fault."

"Isn't her fault?" Elena's voice climbs higher and higher. "She tries to break up my perfect family!"

The gun is shaking against my head now. I close my

eyes and think about all the books I'll never read, all the places I'll never see, all the chances I'll never get.

All because I was stupid enough to fall in love.

Heavy knocking echoes from upstairs.

Elena freezes. My heart pounds even harder than before, nearly exploding from hope.

"Don't make a sound," Elena says, her voice dropping to barely above a whisper. "Either of you. One noise, one whisper, one breath too loud, and I swear on my daughter's life I'll put a bullet in both of your heads."

She pulls the gun away from my head, and I sag forward so hard the ropes cut deeper into my wrists. Blood drips down my hands, but I don't care. I'm alive. For now.

She disappears up the stairs. The basement door closes behind her, but I can tell it's not shut all the way. The darkness isn't nearly as deep as it was before.

In the sudden silence, I can hear everything. Henry's ragged breathing. My own heartbeat pounding in my ears. The sound of Elena's footsteps above us, walking toward the front door.

"What did you do?" I whisper to Henry, my voice barely a breath.

"She found your wedding ring," he groans, and I can hear the pain in every word.

I stare at him through the dim light. "My wedding ring?" It had been hidden carefully away in my bag, I'd thought. ' Why was Elena going through my stuff?"

But before he can answer, a voice drifts down from above.

"Apologies for disturbing you, but we received a call

about a woman who'd been caught with a gun. Would you know anything about that?"

Elena answers, her voice as sweet as honey, like butter wouldn't melt in her mouth. "Officers, I'm so terribly sorry. It was my daughter. She was playing with the phone when I wasn't looking."

It sounds so delusional, there's no way the officers will believe it. At the very least, they would investigate the premises, right? See that Henry and I are being held captive down here?

"We're so sorry for wasting your time," Elena continues, and I can hear the smile in her voice. "I've already had a very serious talk with Sofia about how inappropriate this was. It won't happen again." She continues on, speaking in Portuguese far too quickly for me even have a chance of understanding.

Hope dies in my chest as I realize they aren't coming. And sure enough, after some murmured conversation I can't make out, I hear Elena thank them. Then, the front door slams shut. A moment later, I hear the basement door shutting and the turn of its lock.

In the darkness, I feel Henry's hand brush against mine. His fingers are ice cold, but his touch should be comforting. It's not. Because all it does is remind me that while he's not tied up like me, there's nothing he can do for me. Not with us trapped in darkness behind the locked door.

My throat squeezes in pain again.

I wish she had shot me.

TWENTY-SIX
MORGAN

Life was better when I was single.

There, I said it. I can't believe I'm admitting that, but being tied up here in this basement and staring death in the face, I am.

The truth is, love is messier than I ever imagined it would be. If I had known what things would turn out to be like, I probably never would have signed up for the Eden program. But I had been desperate after James, my ex, dumped me the night I thought he'd propose. And desperate people do desperate things.

I turn toward Henry, whose tired and ragged breathing is the only other sound I hear in the dark. He should have been my salvation, the man who kept me warm and happy and safe through life. And yet, here we are, bound by lies and misplaced trust.

The basement smells like old concrete and something metallic that makes my stomach turn. The cold has seeped into my bones, making every muscle ache worse than it already did.

I should loathe the fact that we're probably going to die together. What was that line the officiant said? Until death do us part? I wonder if this is what he meant; not growing old together in some cozy house with grandchildren running around, but dying together in a madwoman's basement.

Although now that I think about it, he was probably a member of the Eden staff. So he very well knew what until death do we part meant, if I had to guess.

"You okay?" he asks, the shadowed silhouette of his face lifting to meet mine.

"Define okay," I whisper back in a hoarse voice. "Because if okay means tied to a chair in a psychopath's basement, then yeah, I'm fantastic."

He makes a sound that might be a laugh if it weren't so broken. "Fair point."

The silence stretches between us, heavy with all the things that have gone wrong since I found out the truth on the island. I close my eyes and let my head fall back against the chair. Every muscle in my body aches, my wrists are raw from the rope, and my leg is throbbing again from when Genevieve shot me. The pain reminds me of how quickly paradise can turn into hell.

But it's my heart that hurts the most.

"I keep thinking about something Elena said," I murmur into the darkness. "About Genevieve. She called her Eve."

"What about it?"

"How does she know her?" I shift in the chair. "It doesn't make sense."

He shrugs.

"You really don't remember?"

He's quiet for a long moment. I can hear him breathing, almost feel him straining his mind for some memory that would help us figure out what the hell's going on. But maybe the fall from the cliffside really did damage him more than we know, because a few minutes later, his shoulders slump in defeat. He remembers nothing.

"I should have known," I mutter as I look away from him

"Known what?"

"That I couldn't trust you."

"That's not true."

"I'm tied to a chair in a basement, Henry."

This time, he doesn't respond. He gets up with a grunt and starts moving around.

"What are you doing?"

"Looking around. Trying to see if there's anything over here we can use to break out." His voice grows more distant as he moves away from me. "Hang on, these boxes over here. They're full of pictures."

"Pictures?"

"Yeah, framed ones. Just stacks and stacks of them." I hear him lifting something, glass clinking against glass. "Wait a minute..."

"What are they of?"

"I can't see them well enough in this light, but..." he pauses. I hear him rifling through something, then he stops completely. "It's nothing."

"Henry?"

"I told you, it's nothing."

But something in his tone tells me he's not telling me

the truth. Again. I close my eyes and feel the familiar sting of tears. Here we are, possibly about to die, and he's still hiding things from me.

"You know what?" I say, and there's steel in my voice now. "I'm done with this."

"Done with what?"

"This thing where you lie to me. I'm so sick and tired of it, Henry."

The cane taps closer toward me. "Morgan—"

"No. You listen to me." My voice cracks, but I push through. The words have been building inside me for so long, and if we're going to die down here, he's going to hear them. "Love isn't the few scraps of honesty you show scattered among the sea of lies. This, what you're doing and have been doing, isn't love."

I take a shaky breath, feeling tears start to fall again. But these aren't the helpless tears I've been crying for hours. These are angry.

"Do you know what it's like?" I continue, my voice gaining strength. "To love someone who constantly feeds you half the story? Who only gives you half the man, and half the marriage you thought you signed up for?"

The basement falls silent except for our breathing. I can hear my own heartbeat in my ears.

When Henry speaks again, his voice is softer, more vulnerable than I've ever heard it.

"You're right."

The simple admission catches me off guard.

"I'm an awful husband. I lie to you, and... you deserve better than me." He pauses. Then I hear the tap of his cane again, coming closer. "I have an idea about how to get you out of that chair."

I blink, caught off guard by the sudden shift in topic. "What? How?"

"My cane. If I can leverage it against the back of your chair, I might be able to break the wood." I hear him testing the chair, running his hands along the back. "This thing's old. The joints feel loose."

"And then what?"

"And then we figure out why there's photos of me and Eve down here. That's all the box is full of."

My brow furrows. Why would Elena be keeping boxes of their photos down here? Henry misinterprets my expression, because his face falls.

"Morgan, look... I'll do better. I'll... I'll even try therapy."

Laughter bubbles up from somewhere deep inside me, starting as a tremor in my chest before exploding out in a sound that surprises us both. The idea of going through therapy with Henry, after everything we've endured with the Eden program? It's absurd.

When the laughter finally subsides, I ask, "I don't need therapy with you. I need partnership. Honesty. Respect."

"I understand. I haven't done a good job of giving you that, but I promise, I'm going to do that."

The promise does something to my chest, loosens something that's been tight for a while. It's not everything —we still have so much to work through—but it's a start.

"And you're not hiding any more wives that I should know about?" I ask, half-joking, half-not.

"I hope not," he grumbles. "I didn't even know about Elena."

"Okay. But if you are, then nothing Genevieve or Elena's done will even compare to what I'll do to you."

I feel his hand over mine. "I'm not."

"Good. Then get me out."

I hear him positioning himself behind me, the metal tip of his cane scraping against the floor as he finds the right angle. His hands brush against my shoulders as he works, and even in this horrible situation, his touch is comforting.

"This might hurt a little," he warns.

"Everything hurts right now," I tell him. "Just do it."

He places the cane against the chair back, and I feel the pressure as he starts to apply leverage. The wood creaks ominously, and I hold my breath.

The chair back snaps with a crack that echoes through the basement like a gunshot. The sudden release sends me pitching forward, my bound hands still tied to the broken chair back, but I'm free from the seat. The relief is immediate and overwhelming.

"Did it work?" Henry's voice is breathless with exertion.

I flex my fingers, feeling circulation return to my hands as the rope loosens. "It worked."

His hands work quickly at the remaining ropes, sliding the broken chair backing out from behind me. Without the rest of the chair to hold everything in place, the knots come loose easier.

My shoulders scream in protest as I try to move them

for the first time in hours, but the pain is nothing compared to the relief of finally being able to move.

When I finally stand on shaking legs, Henry is there immediately, his hands steadying me as I sway.

"Easy," he says. "Take your time."

But I don't want to take my time. I want to feel human again, want to feel like myself again. I turn toward him in the darkness, and suddenly we're reaching for each other. His arms wrap around me like he's afraid I might disappear.

"I'm sorry," he whispers. "For everything."

"I'm not. Just count yourself lucky I didn't get the chance to shoot you."

"Trust me, I do," he says with a smile I can feel. He runs a hand over my hair and clutches me tighter. "We're going to be okay."

And you know what? I think he might be right. Because here's what I've learned in this basement, tied to that chair with nothing but my thoughts and my fear and my anger: Nothing good ever comes easy. If I want something that'll last, something I can build a foundation on that'll endure, it'll require fighting for it. Fighting for each other, instead of against each other. Not being desperate to find a perfect situation, but making the best of what we have.

And as much as I hate to admit it—as much as he infuriates me with his secrets and his lies—I love him. I despise parts of him, but I love this complicated, damaged, secretive man who somehow found his way into my heart despite having had every opportunity to break me.

The moment stretches between us, warm and real and fragile. But then I remember where we are, why we're here, and my eyes drift toward the direction of the boxes Henry mentioned.

My stomach drops. I cross the room carefully, feeling my way in the darkness until my hands find the boxes. I reach down and grab one of the framed photos, then make my way toward the stairs where the tiniest sliver of light filters through beneath the locked door.

I hold the frame up to catch what little light there is. It's still mostly shadow, but I can see just enough to make out the image. Genevieve's smiling face, Henry's arm around her shoulder in what looks like a casual, intimate pose.

I stare at the photo. Something's nagging at me. The pose looks familiar, but I can't quite place why.

"What do you remember about Cascais?" I ask Henry.

"I remember... it's there at the edge of my grasp. Like I know I should remember, but I just can't."

"You don't remember anything? How did you know I was going to be here then?"

"Well, I remember our conversation about Cascais being one of my favorite places, and it is. And then.... Well, then I remember that I was worried about what you'd find here, because..." his voice trails off.

"Because what?"

"Because I thought I lived here with Eve. And I was worried that you'd be upset when you found our stuff."

My gaze falls to the photo in my hands. "Stuff like pictures?"

"Yeah."

I swallow hard, my heart starting to race as the pieces click into place. "And you're positive you don't remember Elena?"

"It's been so long since I was here. Everything's fuzzy. But..."

"But what?"

He holds his hands up to his head, his fingers massaging his temple. "She's familiar, I know that much."

I frown, and look down at the photo again. A crazy thought comes to mind, and the longer I think on it, the more the hairs rise along the back of my neck. "Henry?"

"Yeah?"

I pause, my voice barely a whisper. "What if it's not real?"

He comes and stands next to me, the soft tap of his cane echoing around us. "What do you mean it's not real?"

"What did she say earlier? 'There is no Eve. Just her. I'm Henry's wife?' Something like that?" My heart begins to race, pounding hard enough that I know I'm onto something huge. "The photos upstairs, over the fireplace mantel... Henry, they're in the exact same pose as this one." His arm over her shoulders, her hand on his chest, the beach in the background.

"I don't get it."

I hold up the frame, my hands trembling. "These photos are the same as the ones upstairs, except instead of you and Genevieve, it's *Elena*."

"What're you saying?"

"I'm saying that none of this is real."

TWENTY-SEVEN
MORGAN

"That can't be true."

Henry's pacing back and forth, tapping his cane nervously against the ground. He's shaking his head, struggling to come to terms with what I'm saying.

"It has to be. It's the only thing that makes sense."

"Except for one thing, Morgan. *Sofia.*"

I hesitate, realizing he's right. Sofia seems to be the spitting image of Henry. Maybe not her face or anything like that, but certainly in her eyes. I lower the photograph. Was it possible that Henry cheated on Genevieve while he was here, met Elena on one night out on the town and left her pregnant and obsessed with him?

I suppose so. It'd explain Sofia's existence. I open my mouth to ask him if it was something he would have done, only for my breath to catch in my throat at the sound of footsteps above. They're lighter, softer, but they're approaching the door.

"Quick, take this!" Henry hisses.

A broken chair leg is shoved into my hands and I grip

it, my knuckles white as I brace myself to fight for my life. Behind me, Henry holds another chair leg in one hand, while he leans on his cane with the other. He's in rough shape, after how Elena booted him down the steps and pistol-whipped him. He knows that of the two of us, I stand the better chance in a fight. But I'm under no delusions that a fight wouldn't last long if Elena had the gun with her.

My thoughts are interrupted by the sound of the lock turning. It clicks, and a second later, the door creaks open. I draw the chair leg back, ready to swing it. A bead of sweat drips down my brow. I lick my lips nervously, and I wait.

Then a shadow passes into the light spilling through the opening.

It's Sofia.

The tension leaves my body like air from a punctured balloon. I lower the makeshift weapon, my shoulders sagging with relief. Sofia stands at the top of the stairs, her small silhouette framed by the light from the hallway above. Her gray eyes are wide with something that looks like fear as she takes in the sight of us—Henry leaning heavily on his cane, both of us clutching broken chair legs like clubs, the splintered remains of my chair scattered across the basement floor.

"Are you okay?" she whispers in her careful English.

Henry and I exchange a glance. I nod first, then he does the same, though I can see the pain etched in the lines around his eyes.

"We're okay," I say, trying to keep my voice gentle despite everything. "Are you?"

She nods quickly, then glances over her shoulder toward the hallway behind her. "Come with me," she says, her voice urgent. "Mama is gone, but not for long."

I don't need to be told twice. Henry and I make our way up the stairs as quickly as we can. Sofia waits for us at the top, then closes the basement door quietly behind us.

My gaze immediately falls on the photos by the front door. They look different now that I suspect the truth. I see how they're too perfect, from the smiles to the lighting, even the fact that there's not a single blemish on Elena's skin.

I turn my attention back to Sofia, and crouch down to her level. "Where did she go?"

"I don't know." She looks between Henry and me with those serious gray eyes. "She said she would be back soon."

Henry limps over to the landline phone on the kitchen counter and picks up the receiver. He holds it to his ear for a moment, then shakes his head. "Line's dead."

Of course it is. Elena wouldn't leave anything to chance if she left the house.

"Your cell phone," I say suddenly, turning to Henry. "Do you still have it?"

Henry pats his pockets, then shakes his head. "I don't."

I turn back to Sofia, crouching down to her level. "Sofia, do you know where Papai's phone is?"

Something flickers across Sofia's face. Guilt, maybe, or shame. She looks down at her feet, her small hands twisting together in front of her.

"Sofia?" I press gently. "It's okay. You can tell me."

"I'm sorry," she whispers, so quietly I almost miss it.

"You're sorry? What for?"

She still refuses to meet my eyes. "I got you in trouble."

"You got me in trouble? What do you mean?"

"I stayed in your bed and Mama caught us."

I draw a deep breath and smile gently, running my hand over her shoulder. "That's not your fault."

She shakes her head, her tone insistent. "I did it."

My smile falters. "What are you trying to say?"

"I wanted her to catch us."

"But why?"

"Because I thought... I thought if she caught us, then she'd make you leave. And that you'd be safe."

"Safe? Sofia, what do you mean safe?"

"I didn't want Mama to hurt you. I like you." Her eyes well with tears, and before I can say anything, she starts to cry.

I share a glance with Henry over my shoulder, before drawing Sofia in for a hug. I hold her close to me, partially to comfort her, but also partially so she doesn't see my look of disbelief. I'm not sure what she's been exposed to in this house, but it's becoming very clear to me that she's more aware of what exactly Elena is than I thought.

"It's okay," I tell her, running my hand over her back in an attempt to comfort her. "We are safe. Everything's okay."

She sniffles and nods, holding me tight.

"Sofia, do you have my things? And Papai's things too?" I ask as gently as I can.

She draws back, still not meeting my eyes. "In my room. I... I took them."

"Can you show me?"

She nods and leads us upstairs to her bedroom. She opens her closet and pulls out my battered bag, setting it down on her bed.

"I'm sorry," she says, her voice thick with tears. "I didn't mean to steal. I just... I was scared."

I unzip the bag and rifle through it quickly. My few remaining clothes and toiletries are there, but at the bottom, I find Henry's phone and wallet. Henry reaches for his phone and tries to turn it on, but the battery is dead.

"Do you have a charger?" I ask Sofia.

She nods and reaches into my bag, pulling out Henry's phone charger. Henry plugs it into the wall outlet by Sofia's bed, and we wait for the screen to light up.

"Sofia?"

The sound of Henry's voice draws my attention away from the phone.

"Can you tell me why you gave your mother the ring?"

She looks from Henry to me and back, her eyes full of pain. "I... you're my Papai. I thought if the ring made Mama angry, she would make you go away again. Then you would be safe too. I didn't want her to hurt you."

Her eyes well with tears.

"Sofia? Does she hurt you too?"

Slowly, she nods.

My heart aches for this little girl who's been caught in the middle of Elena's twisted game. I pull her into a hug, and she melts into me like she's been waiting for permission to fall apart.

"It's okay," I murmur into her hair. "Everything's okay."

Over Sofia's head, I meet Henry's eyes. He's watching us with an expression I can't quite read. Pain, maybe, or guilt? I don't know. But he sees that this little girl loves him, and has been trying to protect him in the only way she knew how. We have to get her out of here, away from Elena.

She sniffles over my shoulder, her fingers clutching me like this might be the last time we ever hold each other. "Are you and Papai in love?"

"What?"

She drags a finger across her nose and wipes her tears. "In the books, the princess always gets a ring from the prince."

I smile at the reference and nod, looking at Henry again. "That's right. I did get a ring."

He's hardly a prince. More like a vampire, for all the life that he and his troubles have sucked out of me, but I don't need to tell her that.

The phone finally flickers to life, the screen casting a faint glow in Sofia's room. Henry immediately tries to make a call, but shakes his head in frustration.

"No signal."

My heart sinks.

"We need to get to town," I say, looking between

Henry and Sofia. "Or at least somewhere with better cell service."

Then we hear a sound that makes my blood freeze and sends chills running down my spine: the sound of the front door opening.

Elena's back.

I hold a finger up to my lips, motioning for Sofia to stay quiet, as we listen to Elena move through the first floor. She's moving past the kitchen, past the living room with those perfectly photoshopped pictures on the mantel.

Henry mouths to me, "The basement door."

I nod, understanding what he's trying to tell me. She's going to check to make sure that it's still locked, and when she discovers that it's not…

Her footsteps stop, and a moment of silence stretches through the house.

Then Elena's voice cuts through the silence. "SOFIA!"

Sofia's small body goes rigid with terror, but there's something else in her gray eyes. Before either Henry or I can stop her, she's already wriggled free from my arms and dashed out the door.

"Where is she going?" Henry hisses to me, his eyes wide with panic and worry.

"She's trying to distract her so we can escape."

"SOFIA! COME HERE. AGORA!" Elena's voice rings through the house, filled with none of the sweetness and love that I'm used to when she's calling for her daughter.

Through the house, we hear Sofia's small footsteps on

the stairs hear her voice calling out innocently: "Mama? What's wrong?"

My fingernails dig into my palms and I bite into my lip, hard enough that I taste the metallic trickle of blood. The survivor in me says to take the opportunity and *run*. But I can't. It's wrong. And judging by the look in Henry's eyes, I know he's thinking the same thing.

We have to save her.

TWENTY-EIGHT
MORGAN

Henry and I move to the window. It's the only way out without having to go into the hallway and risk being overheard by Elena downstairs. I unclasp the latches and lift it, sticking my head out. The night air hits my face, carrying the salt scent of the ocean far below.

I've never been good at judging distance, but I know that it's a hefty drop. The terrace is maybe twelve feet down, and there's nothing beneath us except for manicured grass that looks deceptively soft from up here. But I know it won't be enough to keep the fall from breaking something important.

"What's the plan?" Henry asks, his voice barely above a whisper.

"We need to get Sofia away from her. That's it."

"So we need a distraction then."

"Yeah."

The muscles in Henry's jaw flex as he nods, and I can see him calculating something behind his eyes. "I'll handle the distraction. You get Sofia."

"But—"

Henry shakes his head, refusing to even hear my objection. He takes my hand, his fingers surprisingly warm despite everything. "Listen, there's not much time. You know Sofia better than I do, and if something goes wrong, Elena will go easier on me than you."

"There's no way you can know that for certain."

He gives me a look that's part grimace, part smile. "I do know. She's obsessed with me, right? That has to count for something." He glances at the drop below us, then back at me. "Just do me a favor. Don't lock your knees when you jump. Tuck and roll with it, okay? I don't think a couple with matching canes would make for a great escape story."

I stare at him, hardly believing he's actually making jokes right now. Here we are, about to make a desperate play to escape a woman who's held us captive in her basement, and he's cracking jokes. It's infuriating.

But as much as I want to argue, as much as I want to find some better plan that doesn't involve leaving him alone with Elena, the truth is staring me in the face: he's right. Elena might be obsessed enough to hesitate before putting a bullet in Henry, but she's already proven she has no such qualms about me. And Henry has this infuriating way of being able to talk his way out of just about anything.

I draw a deep, nervous breath. "Okay, fine. Just be careful."

"Don't worry," he says with a forced smile. "I'll do my bit and get away. I'd rather not find out exactly how deep

Elena's obsession with me runs." His attempt at lightness doesn't quite mask the fear in his eyes.

From downstairs, we hear Elena's voice again, sweeter now but with that dangerous edge that makes my skin crawl: "Sofia, querida, are you sure you don't know where they went? It's very important that you tell Mama the truth."

And Sofia, God bless her brave little heart: "I was playing, Mama. I didn't hear anything."

"You know what happens when you lie to Mama, right? I'll have to put you in timeout in our special place."

Suddenly, I understand why there's a chair with ropes in the basement.

Henry squeezes my hand once, then releases it. "Go. I'll give you sixty seconds, then I'm making enough noise to wake the dead."

I swing my leg over the windowsill, my heart hammering against my chest. The ground looks even farther away from this angle, and I have a brief, terrifying vision of landing wrong and breaking my neck before I can help anyone.

But then I think of Sofia downstairs, lying to protect us with the kind of courage that puts adults to shame, and I know I don't have a choice.

I push off from the window ledge and drop.

The wind rips through my hair, strands whipping across my face as I fall. As I said, I'm not good at judging distances, but the fall seems to last forever. Until it doesn't.

I land with a jarring impact that explodes through my body like a bomb. Every bone, every muscle, every nerve ending screams in protest as the earth slams into me with brutal finality. I remember at the last moment to tuck and roll, and as I do, the ground catches my shoulder with a sickening crunch that sends lightning bolts of agony down my arm. My teeth clack together so hard I taste blood, and I'm pretty sure I've chipped something. Then I finally stop rolling and come to rest on my back, gasping and staring up at the endless blue sky.

The sun's warmth dances over my skin. It's a cloudless day; the sort of day where I'd love to find myself outside with a book in hand, maybe lounging by that perfect infinity pool with nothing more pressing to worry about than whether I want iced tea or lemonade. Instead, here I am, trying to survive once again. It's not lost on me that every time I find myself somewhere beautiful—whether it's Eden's island paradise or this stunning Portuguese villa—something terrible ends up happening. It makes me long for the quiet, safe monotony of Des Moines, where the biggest excitement was old Mrs. Henderson arguing with my librarian colleagues about late fees.

Maybe there's something to be said for boring after all.

Sofia's cry echoes from somewhere inside the house, sharp and scared, and it pulls me from my self-pity. As it does, the pain hits with renewed fury, unwanted tears flowing from the corners of my eyes.

I've never been one with a high pain tolerance. Give me a papercut and I'm reaching for the first aid kit. The way that my leg's throbbing now, combined with what feels like a dislocated shoulder and possibly cracked ribs, makes me want to curl up in the grass and die. But that's not an option. Both Sofia and Henry are depending on me to do my part.

With a gasp that sounds more like a sob, I force myself up to my feet. I hobble to the house and lean against the wall, my good hand pressed against the stone as waves of nausea wash over me. I dig my fingernails into my thigh, half out of frustration, half out of desperation to force myself to acclimate to the pain. I can't help anyone if I'm stumbling around.

Then I hear Henry's voice calling out loudly from somewhere inside: "Has anyone seen my phone?"

It's such a mundane question that it has me pause, confused. What is he doing? This is his brilliant distraction plan?

But then I hear Elena's voice call out: "Henry?"

"Elena!" Henry calls back. God, he actually sounds like he's happy to hear her voice. "Good, you're here. I thought I left it charging somewhere."

The genius of it hits me all at once. He's not trying to create chaos or drama. He's playing confused, harmless, leaning into his supposed amnesia.

I hear the tap-tap-tap of Henry's cane moving around upstairs, Elena's voice following him, and I finally get my chance.

Moving as quietly as I can despite the pain screaming through every step, I make my way to the front door. It's unlocked. I push it open carefully, wincing as it creaks slightly.

Sofia is standing at the bottom of the grand staircase, her small face tilted up toward the sounds coming from above. She looks so tiny in this massive house, so vulnerable.

I catch her attention and motion frantically for her to come to me. Her gray eyes go wide when she sees me, and she glances up the stairs once more toward where Henry's voice continues to drift down: "What's wrong? Why do you look so upset?"

Sofia makes her decision. She runs to me on silent feet, and I grab her hand with my good arm.

"We have to go," I whisper. "Right now."

She nods, trusting me completely, and together we slip out the front door and run for the gate as fast as my battered body will allow.

TWENTY-NINE
HENRY

I've always hated when characters in movies act dumb to draw attention to themselves. But I can't deny the effect that it's having on Elena. She's standing in the doorway, one hand folded behind her back like she thinks I don't know that she's got that gun on her; the one that originally belonged to Eve. And me? I'll do whatever it takes to not get shot again.

I blink like a fool, hoping it's convincing enough. "What do you mean where's Morgan?"

Elena draws a sharp breath through her nose. I can tell I'm testing her patience. But what's she supposed to do? She knows that I might suffer from amnesia. And well, she loves me, right? Let's just hope she loves me enough. "Henry, you and Morgan were locked in the basement. Where is she?"

I shake my head and cross the room, pressing my hands against her shoulders. "I understand the basement part, my love. But it's the Morgan part that has me confused. Who are you talking about?"

Her eyes narrow. "Don't act stupid."

Shoot, I've got to lean into this. If I fail, well... like I said, I'd do anything to avoid getting shot again. I let slip some of my anger, furrowing my brows and standing over her. I grip my cane with white knuckles and clench my jaw. "What did you say?"

Elena blinks, suddenly realizing that perhaps there is something wrong with me. She opens her mouth to speak, but I cut her off.

"I have the worst migraine you can possibly imagine. There's a lump the size of a baseball on the back of my head, and I don't even know how it got there." I press my free hand to my temple, which isn't entirely an act. My head *is* pounding. "It's giving me a migraine so bad I can barely think straight. I can hardly remember what happened today, or what day it even is. All I want is to find my phone and call a doctor, and you're badgering me about some random lady named *Morgan?*"

I stuff my hands in my pockets, suddenly needing my cigarettes. My fingers find the crumpled pack of Camels, and I pull them out to discover they're completely destroyed. Crushed beyond saving. That part actually does piss me off, and the frustration bleeds into my voice.

"And now my cigarettes are ruined too. Perfect. Just perfect.'

Elena stares at me, clearly conflicted. I can see the wheels turning behind her eyes, trying to reconcile the man she wanted to punish with this confused, irritable version standing in front of her. Her grip on whatever she's hiding behind her back loosens slightly.

"Henry..." she says softly, and there's genuine concern

in her voice now. I can still see that she loves me, twisted as that love might be. "You really don't remember? The woman who's been staying here? You'd given her a wedding ring?"

I shake my head, making sure to look genuinely bewildered. "A wedding ring? Elena, *you* are my wife. What are you *talking* about?"

Something shifts in her expression. Relief mixed with worry. She runs a hand through her hair, clearly torn between suspicion and the desire to believe me.

"Don't worry about Morgan," she says finally, her voice taking on that dangerous sweetness again. "I'll handle her myself. You need to lie down. You look terrible."

She reaches for my arm, trying to guide me toward what I assume is the bedroom, but I resist at first, playing up the confusion.

"I don't want to lie down. I want answers. I want my phone. I want to know why my head feels like someone took a baseball bat to it."

"Henry, please." There's genuine pleading in her voice now. "You must have hit your head against something."

Never have I felt like strangling someone as much as I did then. Hit my head against something? She *pistol-whipped* me.

"Let me get you some medicine. Some proper painkillers. You'll feel better, and then we can talk about everything."

I let her pull me slowly down the hallway, making sure to walk as slowly as possible, leaning heavily on my cane and stopping every few steps to touch my head or look around like I'm trying to orient myself.

"I'm sorry," I say quietly as we move. "I'm sorry for yelling at you. I just... I can barely remember what's going on. Everything feels wrong, and I can't figure out why."

"It's okay," she murmurs, her free hand rubbing small circles on my back. "It's going to be okay. I'll take care of everything."

Good. The longer I can keep her focused on me, the more time Morgan has to get Sofia out of here. And maybe, if I play this right, I can get that gun away from her and shut this whole nightmare down once and for all.

But suddenly, she tenses.

I glance up at her to see what's wrong, only to see her entire body go rigid. I follow her line of sight, and just barely visible through the massive window that overlooks the front entrance are Morgan and Sofia sprinting across the manicured lawn toward freedom.

"You *liar*," Elena seethes, whipping around to face me. Her eyes burn with pure hatred, all pretense of love and concern evaporating in an instant. She reaches for her gun, and I throw the whole of my weight against her, slamming her into the wall hard enough to rattle the framed photos of me, her, and little baby Sofia.

You'd think that at my height and weight, I'd be able to easily overpower her. But she's surprisingly strong and vicious for someone who's spent her life in the lap of luxury.

Of course, it doesn't help that I'm still weakened from the time I'd spent in recovery with the doctor and from the beating I'd taken in the basement. Or that she's fighting like a woman with everything to lose.

We crash into the hallway wall, then ricochet off it as we grapple for control. She's clawing at my face with her free hand while trying to bring the gun around with the other. I grab her wrist, trying to keep the barrel pointed away from both of us.

"You were supposed to love me!" she screams, her voice raw and desperate. "You were supposed to come back to me!"

We stumble backward into the bedroom, still locked together, still fighting. My cane goes flying, clattering uselessly across the hardwood floor. Without it, my injured leg gives out and we both go down hard, hitting the ground with a bone-jarring impact that drives the air from my lungs.

The gun skitters across the bedroom floor, spinning away from both of us.

We both scramble toward it at the same time, crawling desperately across the polished floor. Elena gets there first, her fingers closing around the grip, but I tackle her again before she can bring it to bear. We roll across the floor, knocking over a chair, sending picture frames crashing from the nightstand.

All those perfect photos of our fake life together, scattered and broken on the floor.

Elena brings her knee up hard into my ribs, and I grunt in pain but don't let go. I can't let go. If she gets control of that gun, I'm dead. And Morgan? She'll end up in the ground right next to me.

"Let go!" Elena shrieks, her eyes wide and unhinged. "LET GO!"

I twist her wrist, trying to force her to drop the weapon, and she screams in fury and pain. We're both breathing hard, both bleeding from various scratches and impacts, both fighting with the desperation of people who know this is it—winner takes all, loser takes a bullet.

Then with a final scream, she wraps her finger around the trigger and pulls.

The gun goes off.

THIRTY
MORGAN

All I can hear beyond the roar of the wind in my ears is the sound of my own labored breathing, my lungs working at overcapacity as I push my battered body harder than it's ever been pushed. Saliva fills my mouth as I sprint toward the front gate, Sofia's small hand clutched desperately in mine.

There's a stitch forming in my side that feels like someone's driving a knife between my ribs, but I push the pain aside. I'm not an athlete, and I never will be. But it's moments like these that have me promising myself I'll take up running later. That is, assuming there *is* a later.

But we're so close to safety now, so close to freedom. The ornate iron gate looms ahead of us, and I can see the narrow road beyond it that leads down into town. We reach the gate and I slide it open with shaking hands, the metal protesting with a rusty screech. I push Sofia through the opening first, making sure she's clear before I start to squeeze through myself.

That's when I hear it: the sharp crack of a gunshot echoing from inside the house.

The sound stops me dead in my tracks. Sofia's eyes widen in absolute terror as her gaze flicks from me back to the house, her small body beginning to tremble uncontrollably.

I know exactly what she's thinking because the same horrible questions are racing through my own mind.

Is it Henry who's been shot? Is he lying bleeding on Elena's perfect floors while she stands over him with that gun?

But I can see in Sofia's gray eyes—Henry's eyes—that there's something even more complicated tearing her apart. For whatever cruel punishments her mother has subjected her to, there is still love there; the kind of complicated, desperate love that exists between a mother and child even when that mother is a monster.

And Henry? He's the father she's dreamed about, someone who existed more as an ideal than a real person until he walked back into her life. Now that ideal might be shattered, might be bleeding out on a bedroom floor.

"Papai," she whispers, the word so quiet I almost miss it over the sound of my own ragged breathing.

I want to take her to safety, and leave Henry behind. Since the moment he entered my life, it has been absolute hell.

But while every survival instinct in my body screams for me to run with Sofia and to forget about him, my heart calls back to the man in the house. He's the one who volunteered to distract Elena so that I could get away with Sofia. And now it's my turn to help.

I kneel down in front of Sofia and take her hands in mine. "Sofia?" She's still staring at the house, her small face pale with terror. "Sofia, I need you to listen to me."

My words don't seem to reach her.

"Sofia!"

Finally, I break through to her. She meets my eyes, tears streaming down her cheeks. "Is he okay?"

"I'm sure he is," I lie, forcing my voice to stay steady. "But you don't need to worry about him right now. Can you be a big girl and do something for me?"

She nods, her bottom lip trembling as she wrings her hands. "Yes, Tia Morgan. I can."

"Good girl. I need you to run into town and get the police. Tell them we need help at the big white house on the cliff, okay? Can you do that?"

"But what about you? What about Papai?"

"I'm going to help him," I tell her, squeezing her hands. "But I need to know you're safe first. Run as fast as you can, and don't look back. Can you promise me?"

She nods, wiping her nose with the back of her hand. "I promise."

"Go. Now."

Sofia takes off running down the narrow road, her small legs carrying her as fast as they can toward town. I wait until she disappears around the first bend, then I turn back toward the house.

Every survival instinct I have is screaming at me to follow Sofia, to get as far away from this place as possible. But I can't leave Henry. Not after everything we've been through, not after he risked his life to give us a chance to escape.

I slip back through the gate and run toward the house, my injured leg protesting with every step. The front door is still open from our escape, and I crash through it without hesitation. The house feels different now; it's charged with violence, thick with the scent of gunpowder. And perhaps most terrifying of all, it's dead silent.

I fly up the stairs to find the hallway in ruins. The picture frames that had hung from the wall are smashed on the floor, shattered glass strewn across the polished floor.

But it's nothing compared to what I find when I reach the bedroom.

Elena stands in the center of the room, holding the gun with both hands, her arms shaking slightly from the effort. Her perfect hair is a wild mess, strands hanging loose around her face. Her silk blouse is torn at the shoulder, and there's a scratch across her cheek that's bleeding.

Henry is on the floor near the far wall, propped up against the dresser. His face is gray, and there's blood, *so much blood*, spreading across his shirt. He's only just conscious, his eyes drifting back and forth.

"I knew you'd come back," Elena says without turning around, somehow sensing my presence. "You couldn't help yourself, could you?"

I raise my hands slowly, trying to appear non-threatening. "Elena, let's talk about this. Henry needs medical attention—"

"Henry needs to learn his place," she snaps, her voice cracking with emotion. "We all do."

"You're right," I say carefully, taking a small step into

the room. "But if you shoot him, if you hurt him any more than you already have, you'll go to prison. You love him. Don't do this."

Elena laughs, a sound that's half hysteria, half genuine amusement. "You think this is about Henry? You think I'm some lovesick wife who can't let go of him?"

The words steal the breath from my lungs. I blink, because that's *exactly* what I thought. "You're not?"

"God, you're all such fools," Elena says, finally turning to face me. "All of you, believing whatever you wanted to believe. Even you, Henry, with your pathetic amnesia."

Henry's trying to sit up straighter, wincing with the effort. But he fails. Instead, he slides a little further down, his shoulders slumping with exhaustion.

"Elena, what are you talking about?" I ask, growing more worried about him by the moment.

"He was just one piece of a dream. No, that's not right," she says, her voice getting higher, more manic. "*The* dream."

My blood turns to ice.

Elena's eyes go distant, as she stares into somewhere beyond our grounded reality. "All I wanted is to be perfect. To be beautiful and elegant and everything she was."

I don't have to guess twice to know who she's talking about.

"Genevieve?"

Her gaze snaps to mine, and I see it now. How the photos, the house, even *me* dressed and working as her maid, all played into her dream.

"You're insane," I whisper.

"I'm dedicated," Elena corrects. "More dedicated than any of you could ever understand. Do you want to know the truth? The real truth?"

She's enjoying this, I realize. The reveal, the control, the power of holding all the secrets while we fumbled around in the dark.

"I studied her for years," Elena says, her voice dropping to almost a whisper. "I watched how she walked, how she talked, what she wore, who she loved. All of it, to be the most perfect woman to grace this sad patch of earth." She barks in laughter, the sudden sound startling me. "She changed my life."

The hairs along the back of my neck stand, because as disturbing as it is, I can see a part of myself in her. I've felt that envy to match everything that Genevieve was, to have the world swoon over everything that I did. I've felt that sad desperation to love and be loved, and the anger that came with failing to achieve even that, no matter how much effort I put in. In another world, perhaps Elena and I could have been friends, twin souls as we are.

"Elena," Henry rasps. His breathing is worryingly shallow. I need to do something soon.

"I moved into her house," Elena continues, ignoring him. "I took her husband. I created the perfect life she should have had. And then you—" she gestures at me with the gun, "—you ruined everything by showing up here, reminding him of his pathetic fake marriage."

"But Sofia—" I start.

"Sofia isn't mine," Elena says with a casual shrug that makes my stomach turn. "Or Henry's. She belonged to some poor American tourist who... it doesn't matter.

When you're building the perfect life, people are replaceable. *Children* are replaceable."

Oh, my God.

"You kidnapped her," I breathe.

"I rescued her from a life of poverty," Elena snaps. "And if the girl continues to play her part, I'll give her everything that Genevieve's daughter should have had. If not..." she waves the gun casually. "Oh, well."

Oh, *well?*

"You're not Genevieve," I say, my voice shaking with fury. "You're just a sick woman who's so obsessed with someone else's life that you've destroyed everything real in your own."

Elena's face twists with anger. "I AM her! I am *everything* that she is! I'm perfect!"

"No," Henry says weakly from the floor. "You're nothing like her."

Elena swings the gun toward him, her finger tightening on the trigger. "Don't you dare speak about her like you knew her better than I do!"

Henry's breathing is getting more labored, but something shifts in his expression. Despite the pain, despite the blood loss, there's a clarity in his eyes I haven't seen before.

"You want to know about Genevieve?" he says. "The real Genevieve?"

Elena's grip on the gun wavers slightly. "Shut up."

"She was cruel," Henry continues, pushing himself up against the dresser despite the obvious agony it causes him. "She was manipulative. She played games with people's lives because she was bored. She made me feel like I was going insane half the time."

"That's not true!" Elena shrieks, but I can see uncertainty flickering in her eyes. "Mentiras! Todas mentiras!"

"She was petty and jealous and vindictive," Henry goes on, his voice getting stronger even as his body gets weaker. "She wasn't perfect, Elena. She was deeply, fundamentally flawed."

Elena's face contorts with rage. "You're lying!"

"And you know what?" Henry's eyes find mine across the room. "If you really wanted someone perfect—someone with imperfections that somehow make them everything they should be—you should have tried to be more like Morgan."

I stare at him, my heart skipping a beat. Even now, bleeding and possibly dying, he's still trying to protect me in his own twisted way.

"She's kind without being weak. She's strong without being cruel. She loves without trying to destroy." He pauses, and smiles. "Morgan is everything Genevieve ever wished she could be."

Something in Elena snaps. The careful mask I've seen her wear all this time has finally, irreversibly, cracked.

"NO!" she screams, swinging the gun wildly between Henry and me. "I AM PERFECT! I AM—"

This is my chance. Maybe my only chance.

I lunge forward, grabbing for the gun just as Elena pulls the trigger. The shot goes wide, the bullet embedding itself in the wall near an antique lamp. The lamp explodes in a shower of sparks and glass, and somehow—impossibly—the wiring behind it ignites.

Elena and I hit the ground hard, rolling across the floor as we fight for control of the weapon. She's stronger than I expected, fueled by absolute madness, but I have desperation on my side. The desperation of someone who refuses to die in this house, in this woman's twisted fantasy.

The smell of smoke fills the air almost immediately.

I manage to get my hands on the gun and wrench it away from Elena, sending it skittering across the floor and under the bed. Elena claws at my face, screaming incoherently, but I can see the flames already licking at the wallpaper behind her.

"The house is on fire!" I shout, rolling away from her. "We have to get out!"

But Elena isn't listening. She's staring at the flames with a look that's half horror, half fascination.

"Não," she whispers. "Não pode ser assim. This is all wrong. This isn't how it's supposed to end."

I scramble over to Henry, who's barely conscious now. The blood loss is getting to him, and the smoke isn't helping.

"Henry, we have to go. Now."

He nods weakly, trying to push himself up. I get my arm under his shoulder and start hauling him toward the door.

I look back at Elena, who's now standing in the middle of the room as flames spread up the walls around her. She's not trying to escape. She's just standing there, watching her perfect world burn.

"Elena, come on!" I shout at her. "You have to get out!"

She turns to look at me, and her expression is eerily calm. "Leave? And go where? This is Eve's house. This is where I belong. Where I've always belonged."

The flames are getting higher, the smoke thicker. I can barely breathe, and Henry's getting heavier against my side.

"Elena!"

But she shakes her head, turning back to face the fire. "If I can't be perfect here, then I don't want to be anywhere else."

She's choosing to stay. She'd rather burn with her fantasy than face reality without it.

I shake my head and drag Henry out of the bedroom and into the hallway, but the stairs are already blocked by flames that have spread down from the second floor. The old house is going up like a torch.

"The window," Henry gasps, pointing weakly toward the master bedroom's balcony. "Pool's right below."

I look back at the bedroom, where Elena is still standing motionless as fire consumes everything around her. For a moment, I consider trying to force her out, but Henry's weight is pulling me down and I can hear shouting in the distance.

We make it back to the balcony, but then Henry suddenly rips himself free from my grasp. He drops to the floor, just as a wave of heat rolls out. I hold my hand up, held at bay for a moment by the unbearable heat.

"Henry!" I scream.

But he's crawling back into the fire. I grab a hold of his feet and pull him back, only for him to kick me off.

"What are you doing?"

He reaches for something underneath the bed, straining his arm and screaming as the flames lick across the side of his shoulder. Then, finally, he relents and calls for my help.

I dash in and grab his arm, pulling him to his feet and rushing back out onto the balcony, smoke rising from the both of us.

"Hold on," I tell him, and we climb over the balcony railing together.

The drop to the pool seems endless, and for a moment I'm falling through space with Henry's weight pulling us both down. Then we hit the water with a tremendous splash that drives the air from my lungs.

When I surface, gasping and coughing, Henry is floating beside me, barely conscious but alive. I hold him to me and swim to the pool's edge, dragging him out just as the entire second floor erupts in flames.

That's when Elena's screams begin.

They pierce the air, rising above the roar of the fire and the wail of the approaching sirens. It's a sound of pure anguish, the sound of someone watching their entire world—their entire identity—burn to nothing.

I don't think I'll ever forget that sound. Even now, as police cars and fire trucks come screaming up the other side of the house, as paramedics rush toward us, as Sofia comes running from the first police car with tears streaming down her face, Elena's screams fill the air.

And then, suddenly, they stop.

The silence that follows is somehow worse than the screaming.

Henry's hand finds mine as the paramedics work on his wounds, as Sofia clings to me and police officers ask us questions we're not ready to answer yet.

Behind us, the house where Elena tried to build her beautiful perfect life, burns against the sun. And somewhere in those flames is a woman who chose her delusions over reality, right up until the very end.

The police will have questions. There will be investigations, trials, explanations that will never fully capture the horror of what happened here.

But for now, we're alive. Somehow, impossibly, we're alive.

And Elena's perfect world is nothing but ash and smoke on the wind.

THIRTY-ONE
MORGAN
3 MONTHS LATER

The backyard of our little house in Des Moines isn't much to look at; it's just a patch of grass surrounded by a chain-link fence, with our neighbor's vegetable garden visible on one side and the Johnsons' above-ground pool on the other. But with white folding chairs arranged in a small semicircle and string lights draped between the oak trees, it feels perfect.

More than perfect, actually.

Henry had wanted to buy something grand: a mansion with sprawling grounds and a view of the river, but I'd insisted on this modest two-bedroom in a normal neighborhood. After everything we'd been through, normal was exactly what I needed.

I smooth down the simple white dress I found at a thrift store downtown. Something that makes me feel more myself than I've felt in a long while. My injured leg still aches when I stand too long, and there's a scar on my shoulder from the fall that will probably never completely fade. But I'm alive. We're alive. And after everything we've been through, that feels like nothing short of a miracle.

Of course, we'll forget what happened in Cascais. Shortly after the fire, when we were at Café do Horizonte celebrating the simple fact that we survived another psychopath, Henry finally remembered where he knew Elena from. She had been his and Genevieve's maid for all of two weeks. And just like me, she had worn that silly maid dress at Genevieve's request.

"You ready for this?" Tiana asks, adjusting the small bouquet of wildflowers in my hands. She and Janet from the library drove over together, both of them still barely able to believe the whole story I'd told them about the island and Portugal. Well, the edited version anyway, which included nothing of Eden. Some truths are too dark for a wedding day.

"More than ready," I tell her, and I mean it.

Henry stands at the makeshift altar we've set up near the back fence, leaning slightly on his cane but looking stronger than he has in months. The physical therapy has been grueling for both of us, but we're healing, inside and out

The doctors said he'd always walk with a limp now, that the damage to his hip was too extensive to heal completely after repeated injuries, even with his access to state-of-the-art healthcare. But he's here, and he's mine, and that's all that matters.

Sofia bounces on her toes beside him, wearing a yellow sundress that makes her gray eyes sparkle. The custody proceedings had been complicated, particularly because the Cascais authorities couldn't trace any of

Sofia's remaining relatives. But with Henry's money, we were able to smooth the process along so that we could adopt Sofia formally.

"Ladies and gentlemen," Henry calls out, his voice carrying easily across our small gathering. "Thank you all for being here today. I know this isn't exactly a traditional wedding ceremony—"

"Given that you're already married," Janet calls out, making everyone laugh.

"Technically married," I correct, grinning at her. "But that was under false pretenses. This time, we're doing it right, and I'm getting that man's vows."

Henry's eyes find mine across the small space, and the look in them makes my heart skip just like it did that first day on the island. Before Eden, before Elena, before everything went so terribly wrong and somehow came out right anyway.

"Morgan," he says, his voice soft but carrying clearly in the evening air. "When I first saw you, I thought I was the luckiest man alive. I was wrong."

I raise an eyebrow, and he grins.

"I was luckier than that. Because you didn't just become my wife. You became my partner in survival."

At that, I laugh. It's a joke that goes over the heads of anyone else present, but that's okay. Some things are better kept between us. Tears blur my vision, but I don't look away from his face.

He shifts from one foot to the other, leaning more heavily on his cane. As he speaks, his voice grows rougher with emotion. "I know I put you through hell. I know there were times when loving me felt like the worst decision you'd ever made. But you stayed. You fought for us when I couldn't fight for myself. And now I get to spend the rest of my life trying to be worthy of that faith."

"You already are," I whisper, but he shakes his head.

"No, but I will be. Every day, for the rest of our lives, I will be."

Sofia steps forward then, carefully carrying a small velvet box. She opens it with the seriousness of someone handling precious treasure, and my breath catches in my throat.

It's my ring. The ring Henry gave me on the island, the one Elena took from me, the one I thought was lost forever in the fire that consumed the house.

"How—?" I start, but Henry's already reaching for my hand.

"I grabbed it from the bedroom before we jumped," he says. He lifts the ring from Sofia's careful fingers. "I know what this means to you. Another ring wouldn't be the same."

The diamond catches the light from our string of bulbs, throwing tiny rainbows across my dress. It's the same ring, but somehow it feels completely different now. Before, it was a symbol of a lie, a pretty prop in Eden's elaborate theater. Now it's real. *We're* real.

"Morgan Sloane," Henry says, slipping the ring onto my finger where it belongs. "Will you marry me? Really marry me this time, with real vows and real promises and real love?"

I look around at our small gathering—Tiana and Janet beaming at us, Sofia practically vibrating with excitement, our elderly neighbor Mr. Peterson who wandered over when he heard the music and got invited to stay. This isn't the fairy-tale wedding I used to dream about, with hundreds of guests and a designer dress and flowers that cost more than my monthly salary.

It's better. It's ours.

"You know," I say, loud enough for everyone to hear, "most people take their time getting to know someone before they marry them. But I've always been the type to just marry someone at first sight."

The laughter that erupts from our friends makes my heart soar. Henry throws back his head and laughs too, the sound rich and genuine and absolutely perfect.

"Is that a yes?" he asks when the laughter dies down.

I reach up and cup his face in my hands, feeling the slight roughness of his five o'clock shadow, the warmth of his skin, the absolute reality of him.

"Sim," I say. "Always yes."

When he kisses me, Sofia cheers and claps, and Tiana might be crying, and somewhere in the distance I can hear our neighbor's dog barking at all the commotion. It's chaotic and absolutely nothing like the wedding I thought I wanted.

It's everything I never knew I needed.

As the sun sets over Des Moines and our friends drift toward the folding table laden with catered Chinese and a slightly lopsided cake Sofia helped me make yesterday, Henry pulls me close and whispers in my ear: "Ready to start our real life, Mrs. Langford?"

I lean into him, feeling the solid warmth of his chest against my cheek, hearing the steady beat of his heart that almost stopped beating in that Portuguese mansion.

"I've been ready since the moment I met you," I tell him. And no truer words have ever been spoken.

Sofia runs up and wraps her arms around both of us, and for a moment we just stand there in our little backyard in Iowa, holding each other as the fireflies start to blink on and off in the gathering dusk.

This is home.

And it feels just right.

A LETTER FROM ZIA

Dear Reader,

Originally, this book was never meant to be. I truly thought that The Newlywed would only ever be a standalone. However, there's been so much love coming my way, and such popular demand for a sequel, that this book was something I knew I had to write.

If this was one that you enjoyed, please do consider leaving an honest review on Amazon, Goodreads, TikTok, Facebook, or wherever you are. Or if you'd like, drop me a personal message yourself, and tell me what you think. I always love to hear from readers, and respond to every email.

You can find me at: zia.rayyan.author@gmail.com.

Either way, thank you for giving an indie

author a chance, and I hope you keep on reading my books. Keep an eye out, I've always got a new one coming!

Until next time,
Zia

ALSO BY ZIA RAYYAN

Miss Murder
Mrs. Murder
The Newlywed
The Newlywed's Lie
Mother, Mother

ABOUT THE AUTHOR

Zia Rayyan is a psychological thriller author with no background, no alibi—only a need to write about the lies we tell, and the ones we bury.

You can reach Zia at ziarayyan.com, by email at zia.rayyan.author@gmail.com, or by joining the official Zia Rayyan Facebook Reader Group. Come join the community and hang out!

Printed in Dunstable, United Kingdom